Natural Beauty

Natural Beauty
Leslie DuBois

Natural Beauty Copyright © 2014 Leslie DuBois

Published by Little Prince Publishing in Charleston, South Carolina.
Cover Design: Sybil Nelson
Cover Photo: istockphoto

.

ISBN-13: 978-1-939947-04-8
ISBN-10: 1939947049

Printed in the United States of America
Visit www.LittlePrincePublishing.com

Author's Note – I am not a professional cosmetologist. All of the hair ideas and tips are solely based on personal opinion from the things I have tried on my own hair.

Chapter 1: Relaxed

Relaxer: A chemical process that straightens or 'relaxes' the natural curl pattern of hair. Since a chemical relaxer changes the natural formation of the hair it can be very damaging if done incorrectly or if not properly maintained. The crème or lotion relaxer must be reapplied every 6 to 8 weeks to the new growth of the hair.

~~~

I try to think that I'm not one of those sad, pathetic girls who can't live without a man. The ones that stay with a man they know is no good for them because they're afraid of moving on. Or the ones that try to force or manipulate a man into marrying them because they want the ring and not the actual man. I'm not that kind of girl. Or so I thought.

I had been dating my boyfriend Vinny for seven years and in all that time I had never pressured him into marrying me. Okay, well besides the few comments here and there about where I wanted to live after I got married or how many kids I wanted to have. But those were innocent general statements. I didn't do anything blatant like leave wedding magazines around his apartment. Okay, so I did that *once*, but that was all.

Anyway, all of that was behind me because tonight was the night. I knew it. Vinny had been planning a special dinner for me for over a week. And since it wasn't my birthday and our seven year anniversary was still two months away, I knew it had to be the proposal. Why else would he have called me three times in the last hour to make sure I was still coming? And two weeks ago, he asked for my dad's number at work and then went out to lunch with him. Tonight was the night.

I sat back in my vanity seat in front of my mirror and sipped my pre-dinner wine. I was completely relaxed. I knew he was going to propose and it didn't scare me at all. I loved him and he loved me. I would have married him two days after we met if he'd ask. I was *that* crazy about him.

Of course, he didn't ask then. And in seven years, he had never brought up the word marriage unless I dragged it out of him. The only time we had openly talked about it was four years ago when I jokingly asked when his parents would be signing him up for an arranged marriage.

"Don't joke about that. Arranged marriages are still very common in my culture," he had said. Vinny, or shall I say, Vinyay Gupta was a first generation Indian American. His parents were still in India and had never even been to visit him in this country.

Relaxed

"Fine, all joking aside," I had said. "Are you going to have an arranged marriage one day?"

Instead of answering, Vinny finished off his beer and said, "I gotta take a piss."

And that was the last time we had an actual conversation about marriage. We didn't even discuss it two years ago when he flew to Canada for his sister's wedding. I didn't dare ask whether her marriage was arranged or not.

Of course, I only had his word to go on about the whole arranged marriage thing. He was the only Indian person I knew. I had never met his family so I couldn't verify it with them.

My stomach lurched suddenly. What if this wasn't a proposal? I mean, I had never even met his family. Would someone as traditional as Vinny marry someone without his parents' approval?

I shook off my doubt. Vinny wasn't *that* traditional as evidenced by the amount of pot he smoked on a daily basis. I needed to relax. Speaking of relax, I thought as I leaned toward the mirror. I needed to get my edges done. This weave in my hair probably should have come out a few weeks ago, but I didn't have time to worry about my hair lately. We had a new needy client at work that was sucking away all my free time. As a temporary solution, I picked up my already heated curling iron and straightened my edges. Then I smoothed them down with some gel to cover the tracks in my head.

My cell phone buzzed. It was Vinny… again.

"You in the cab?" he asked.

"Would you chillax?"

"You know no one says chillax anymore, right?"

"And you know no one calls their girlfriend four times in an hour to make sure she's coming to a regular old dinner," I said "This is just a regular dinner, right?"

He paused. I knew I shouldn't have been trying to pump him for information like this, but I couldn't help it. I was too curious.

"Just hurry up and get here," he said effectively avoiding the question.

"Maybe I could hurry up if you would let me get off the phone."

"You mean, you're not in the cab? Mags, seriously? You're supposed to be here in ten minutes."

"Goodbye, Vinyay," I said clicking off the phone.

I was planning on putting some curls in my long weave, but the way he was flipping out, I knew I wouldn't have time. I'd just have to wear it straight. Vinny liked it straight anyway. His favorite hair style of mine was when I had a weave that went all the way to my butt. I didn't think he would stop touching it for the entire three months I had it. I joked that it was probably the hair of one of his cousins in India. He didn't find that funny.

~~~

When I saw Vinny standing in the lobby of the restaurant, I knew it was a special night. He was clean shaven and wearing the suit I bought him when we graduated college four years ago and he needed to go on job interviews. Fortunately for him, he ended up with a job that didn't require dressing up. As a video game designer, he rarely had to get out of his pajamas.

"You look beautiful, baby," he said kissing me and petting my hair.

"So do you."

He smiled shyly showing the dimple in his left cheek. I loved that dimple. It was so sexy.

"You're not supposed to tell a man he's beautiful."

"Well, I can tell my man anything I want," I said kissing him again.

~~~

Dinner was painfully long. Since when did we need to eat a five course meal? Usually, our date nights consisted of ordering pizza and passing a bottle of Pepsi back and forth.

Every time a plate was put before me, I kept checking it to make sure there wasn't a ring hidden in my food.

"What are you doing?" he asked when he caught me once.

"Oh, just making sure there are no...mushrooms in my food."

He looked at me strangely. "That's Bananas Foster."

"You know I hate mushrooms. Can never be too careful."

"Right," he said as he finished his ice cream. When he asked for the check, my heart sank. It wasn't happening.

"Hey, let's go for a walk," he said after he paid the bill.

"A walk?" I said still a little stunned at the lack of a ring on my finger. "Why walk when we can drive?"

"Come on, it's a nice night. It will be romantic."

Romantic? "I started to perk up a bit. Maybe he was going to ask on our walk.

~~~

"Would you slow down? What's the rush?" I said a few minutes later.

"What? Oh yeah, okay," he said slowing his pace. He seemed distracted. And he was walking in an oddly specific direction as if he had a certain place to go.

"I remember this neighborhood," I said, looking around. "We're in Barney." Barney was an old neighborhood of DC that had gone through a major face lift. It now had an air of folk trendiness with a backdrop of beautiful classic brownstone homes.

Vinny and I literally ran across this neighborhood two years ago when we were training to run a marathon together. Of course, after a week of training Vinny decided marathons weren't his thing and went back to his steady diet of marijuana and grilled cheese. I ran the marathon alone.

"Oh, it's the house!" I said as we came across my favorite house in the neighborhood. It was a three story brownstone with a stained glass window in the door. The door frame was painted a warm mahogany brown just like my name. I even loved the ornate red window shutters that gave it a pop of color.

"You still like this house, huh?" Vinny said stopping in front of it.

"Are you kidding? I'm completely in love with this house. You know that."

Relaxed

He turned my face toward his and said, "And I'm completely in love with you." He grasped both my hands and then kissed them.

As he stared into my eyes, I knew this was the moment. I would soon be Mrs. Vinyay Gupta. I took a deep breath and waited for what he would say next.

"I love you more than anything in the world," he continued. "Your happiness means everything to me. This is why I bought you this house."

Still holding my breath, I couldn't say anything. I was still waiting for him to get on one knee and say those four little words. When he didn't and I was about to asphyxiate, I finally breathed and said, "You bought me a house?"

"Well, us. I bought *us* a house. I hoped we could live there together."

I looked back and forth between him and the house. Yes, I loved him and I loved the house. But there was something missing for me.

"So you want us to live together?"

"Yeah!" he said excitedly as he held up a key.

"That's what you are *proposing*?" I put special emphasis on the word proposing. He didn't pick up on it.

"We practically live together already," he said. "Why don't we make it official?"

"And you think this makes it official?"

"Well, yeah. Why not?"

"And this is all you wanted to ask me tonight? There's nothing else?" I asked, hopeful.

"Um, no. Why?"

I rolled my eyes and started walking away.

"Mags, what's wrong?" He stepped in front of me to block my escape.

"Why did you meet with my father two weeks ago?"

"Your dad? Babe, he's a mortgage broker. I worked with him to get the loan for our house."

Why the hell didn't I consider that possibility?

"Maggie, please tell me what's wrong? Don't you want to live with me? Don't you like the house?"

Just then I saw a taxi turn on to the street. I waved it over to me.

"Of course, I like the house. Do you remember what I said two years ago the first time I saw it?"

"You said you could see yourself raising a family there."

"I said I could see myself raising a family there with my HUSBAND. HUSBAND!"

"Oh, my God," he said as recognition finally dawned on him. "You thought I was going to propose."

Vinny wrapped his arms around my waist. I rested my head on his shoulder as the first of many tears began to fall on my cheeks.

"You know I can't marry someone like you. I thought we'd talked about this."

"We did? When did we talk about this?" I wiped tears away just as the cab pulled up next to us.

"I love you, Maggie, but I'm Indian. I can't marry someone like you."

I wiggled out of his arms. "Well, that means you don't really love me, asshole."

Chapter 2: Transition

Transition: A period of time when a person goes from chemically processed hair to natural hair. This is also often referred to as 'growing out the perm'.

~~~

Hair tip #1: There are many ways to transition from relaxed hair. Many people wear braids or wigs for a few months to let their hair grow out. Others go for the big chop. One good style for transitioning is Bantu Knots (See Chapter 11). It helps blend the two textures of hair nicely.

~~~

Someone like me.
Someone like me.
He couldn't marry *someone like me.* Those were the last words he said to me almost a week ago. What the hell did that even mean? Did he mean someone like me as in a beautiful, college educated, independent woman? Because that is what I was. Maybe he didn't see me like that at all.

Could he possibly have meant someone with my skin color? That couldn't be it. We were practically the same shade of brown. And if he happened to spend more time in the sun than I did, he could even be darker than me sometimes.

I set down my glass of wine and stared at myself in the mirror so long that my eyes started to cross. It was like I was staring at one of those magic shape pictures and I was expecting another image to suddenly appear. I knew that wouldn't happen. I was black and I would always be black. The correct term was supposedly African-American though I had never been to Africa a day in my life.

Was race really that important this day and age? I guessed so.

But who cared? So I was black. Did it mean I was less pretty? Did it mean I was less deserving of love somehow? Of course not. I deserved someone who loved me no matter what I looked like. I thought that person was Vinny but I guess I thought wrong.

After I fell in love with Vinny, I never thought I would be at this point in my life. I was supposed to be in the happily ever after stage. I was definitely not supposed to be in this stage of transition. This phase between loves. What if I never fell in love again? What if this was *it* for me?

Speaking of transition, my hair was going through one right now. I had ripped out the long overdue weave the day after Vinny's house proposal. That was the day he had spent banging on my door begging me to let him in after I had the locks changed. I couldn't let him in. I had spent the last seven years letting him into my heart and he had effectively ripped it out of my chest.

He couldn't marry *someone like me*.

Maybe I should have let him explain, I thought feeling the edges of my dry damaged hair. I didn't know whether it was falling out in clumps because I hadn't been taking proper care of it for the past couple of months or because I was so stressed out about my love life.

Love.

I had loved Vinyay Gupta for nearly a quarter of my life. He had bought me a house. He wouldn't have bought me a house if he didn't really love me.

Maybe I was overreacting.

That was the conclusion I came to four days later. After calling in sick all week and not leaving my apartment, I had probably stumbled into an unsafe mental state somewhere between pathetic and hallucinogenic. I thought maybe if I just talked to him, we could work things out. I think really I was starting to panic since he had stopped calling. It had been a full twenty-four hours since his last message on my phone. What if he gave up trying to get me back? I couldn't let that happen. So I slapped on a hat and caught a cab to his apartment in Georgetown.

When I got there, his roommate Anthony opened the door.

"Oh, thank God you're here," he said sweeping me up into a bear hug. "Please take him back. Please say you're here to get back together with him."

Anthony wasn't the touchy-feely type. He was a huge scary looking black guy who used to play football in college. But when he stopped playing, his muscle kind of morphed into fat. He and Vinny had been roommates since senior year and I don't think Anthony had ever given me more than a high five. So now the fact that he was hugging me kind of freaked me out. Too stunned to actually respond I just said, "Huh?"

"He's a broken man, Maggie. Broken and stank. The boy can barely get himself out of bed let alone drag himself to a shower. Do you smell that?" Anthony said waving his arms in the air. "That is the smell of an Indian boy with a broken heart. And let me tell you, it don't smell too good. Just take him back and you two go take a shower together or something."

"Okay," I said still a little taken aback about how forthcoming Anthony was. I wasn't used to him being much of the talkative type.

"He bought you a house. I don't see what the problem is. He loves you. Just take him back. Please. I'm not used to him being around here all the time. He was the perfect roommate when he spent all of his time with you. Now that he's here just whining about how he misses you all day long. I can't take it. I don't think I ever realized how annoying he is. Look, take him back or take me. Yeah, let me move in with you."

"He misses me?" I asked picking up on that one sentence from Anthony's little tirade.

"Yeah, I do." I turned to see Vinny standing in the hallway. He was unshaven and so sloppy he kind of looked homeless. He really was messed up without me.

"I miss you, too," I said running to embrace him.

"I'm so sorry, Maggie. I didn't mean what I said. Of course, I want to marry you."

"You do?"

He nodded.

I wasn't sure if that was a proposal or not. I decided not to assume anything. That was how we had gotten into this mess in the first place.

"Anthony's right. You stink. Why don't you go take a shower and then come to my place?"

Vinny smiled then kissed me. "I love you, Mags."

"I love you, too," I said before he headed to the bathroom.

I turned around to see Anthony plop down on the couch and pick up a game controller. "Thank the Lord," he said as he turned on one of the games Vinny had created. "I knew you two would work it out. Vinny may be lazy, opinionated and have a weird obsession with French rap music, but he is no racist. His best friend is black, his girlfriend is black. I made him an honorary brother years ago." Anthony held up an extra controller and said, "Wanna play?"

I shrugged, grabbed it, and started choosing my character. It was one of those war games where you could only see the character from behind holding a gun so I never understood the point of choosing the character to begin with. I told Vinny this, but he never took my suggestions when he was developing a game.

"And look, once his family sees how crazy he is about you, I'm sure they'll love you too," Anthony added. "They have no problem with me."

"What do you mean?" I asked as I changed my weapon from an AK-47 to a rocket launcher.

"When I met them, they seemed to be fine with my race."

I paused the game. "When did you meet his family?"

"Two years ago right before his sister's wedding. They flew in to DC from India. Then they came by and picked him up on their way to Toronto. Hey, why did you pause it?"

"You met his family two years ago? His family was here two years ago?" I stood and started pacing the room. "So his parents were here in Washington DC. Not only did he not introduce me, but he didn't even tell me they were in the country."

"Oh. You didn't know. I probably shouldn't have said that," Anthony said as it dawned on him what was happening.

"Vinny told me that his parents have never been here," I said, anger welling inside me. "He told me that he would introduce me to his parents the first chance he got. What else has Mr. Gupta lied about?

I stormed down the hall and busted through the bathroom door. After flinging open the shower curtain I yelled, "Your parents were here two years ago?"

"What the hell, Mags?" he yelled trying to cover himself with the curtain. As if he had anything I had never seen before.

"Don't call me that. That's not even my name. It's Mahogany." I don't know why I decided to bring up my proper name at that time. It's not like I ever cared that he called me Mags before. But since he was the one who gave me that nickname, maybe I felt like the name was associated with my time with him. And that time was now over. Forever. "I'm never going to be good enough for your family, am I?"

He went to turn off the water, but didn't answer. I took that as a no and stormed out of the bathroom.

"Maggie, wait," he said following me.

"I told you don't call me that. It's Mahogany."

"Mahogany, please. What do you want me to do?"

"What do I want you to do?" I stopped walking in the living room and turned on him. "How about not lie to me? How about be proud enough of me to introduce me to your family? I bet they don't even know I exist."

Vinny adjusted the towel he had wrapped around his waist. He looked down and wiped water away from his face. I stared at his slim, brown defined chest. It always amazed me how he never worked out and never lifted more than a bag of popcorn on a daily basis, but was still somehow able to keep a nice physique. That annoyed me even more at the moment. I took my eyes off of his chest and waited for a response. None came.

"Seven years, Vinny. Seven years of my life I gave to you. And for what? So you can pretend I don't exist to every person in your life except your roommate? Is he the only one that is allowed to know about me because he's black too?"

Vinny stole a glance at Anthony. Anthony shook his head disapprovingly and then turned around and went back to his war game.

"Why can't things just keep going the way they always have?" he asked.

"Because I'm better than that. That's why. We're done."

Transition over. It was time to move on.

Chapter 3: The Big Chop

The Big Chop: Cutting off all the chemically processed parts of your hair leaving you with only a few inches or less of tightly curled natural hair.

~~~

Hair tip #2: Don't chop off all your hair when you're drunk and pissed at your boyfriend. Correction, ex-boyfriend.

~~~

Sunday morning I woke up on the couch around noon. I saw three empty bottles of Merlot lying on the floor next to me along with a pair of scissors. Looking around I noticed hair. *My* hair everywhere. I touched my head and screamed.

~~~

"All right, what happened? What's going on?" My friend Carnece said in a hushed panicked voice. Carnece and I had been friends since middle school. I think we bonded over our odd names. I went through elementary school with half the kids unable to say my name and the other half shortening it to hog. Carnece hated the fact that her name was a combination of her father's name Carlton and her mother's name Denece but neither one of them were in her life anymore. Her father left when she was an infant and her mother was in jail. She hated her name, but unfortunately she didn't even have a middle name to go by.

Carnece came through the door, threw down an arm full of trash bags and started looking around my apartment suspiciously.

I had called her hysterically crying about my hair a few minutes after I discovered what I had done. Even thirty minutes later, I was still crying too hard to actually speak.

"Calm down. Calm down. We'll take care of it," she said, hugging me.

"We can't take care of it! It's too late. I want to die."

"Don't talk like that. I'm telling you we can handle it." She led me to the couch and sat me down. "Now, tell me. Where is he?"

"Who?" I asked through the tears

"Vinny."

"I don't know." Why did she care about Vinny at this point in time?

"What do you mean you don't know? Were there any witnesses?" she asked.

"Witnesses? No witnesses. I barely even remember what I did. There was no one else here."

"Oh my God. Is he still alive?"

"Still alive? Who?" I asked.

"Vinny?"

24

"Why wouldn't he be alive? Did something happen to him?" I asked as my tears of sadness suddenly melted away into anxiety.

Carnece held up her hands in the international sign for stop. "Okay. Pause. Rewind. What are you talking about?"

"My hair. Can't you see? Look what I did to my hair?"

Carnece looked at my head for the first time. She closed her eyes and took a deep breath and let it out slowly. "Is that what we're talking about? You cut off your hair?"

"Yeah, what did you think it was?"

"Girl, I thought you had done something to Vinny. I was about to help you hide the body."

Carnece and I looked at each other and then busted out laughing.

~~~

"Did you really think I killed him?" I asked a few minutes later while she was inspecting the damage of my self-inflicted haircut.

"I didn't know what to think," she said. "I knew you were really upset about the break up and then you called me and you were hysterical. The only word I could make out was scissors. I thought you might have stabbed him with some scissors."

"Well now I know the depth of our friendship. You were willing to cover up a homicide for me."

"No judge would have convicted you. Well, no female judge anyway. Not after what he did to you. I can't believe it took you seven years to figure out what a racist dick he is."

"Do you really think it's racism?"

"What else can it be, Mahogany?" she asked.

I sighed. She was right. I had just spent seven years of my life with a man who was ashamed to be with a black girl. What was wrong with me? Was my self-esteem that low? How could I not realize it before? In all fairness, he did a great job of covering his true feelings up.

"But why would he be with me in the first place? Why not date an Indian girl if that is the case?"

"Uh, do you remember where you went to school?" Carnece asked as she started cleaning my living room. She stuffed empty wine bottles into her trash bags which apparently we were supposed to use to transport Vinny's body.

She was right. Cobalt University was beyond predominantly white. It was almost completely white. Of the three thousand students there, only thirty seven considered themselves non-white. We all knew each other by name. That was how Vinny and I got to know each other in the first place. Carnece had gone in the complete opposite direction and attended an all-black university. Somehow we remained best friends all through college even though I was in Minnesota and she was in DC.

"But why not break up with me when he realized our relationship wasn't going anywhere. Why put me through seven years of hoping?"

She shrugged and sat down next to me. "Maybe he was hoping too," she said putting her arm around me. "You have to know he really loves you. No one stays with someone for seven years if there isn't some amount of love there. Or money. And it ain't money; I've seen your bank statement. So it's love. But when it comes to race, sometimes love ain't enough."

It was a heartbreaking thought. Vinny didn't love me enough to get over our different races. I couldn't cry anymore, though. I had no more tears. I needed to focus my attention on something else if I was ever going to get through this.

"So what are we going to do about this?" I asked indicating my hair.

Carnece smiled. "I might not be able to fix your relationship problems, but I can definitely hook up your hair."

Chapter 4: Wash N Go

Wash N Go: This is kind of self-explanatory. It's a hair style that requires little effort. You wash it, and you go.

~~~

Hair tip #3: Own it. No matter what your hair looks like, you have to own it. You have to make it seem like whatever is on your head is there because you wanted it like that. If you believe that, everyone else will as well.

~~~

Most of Carnece 'hooking up' my hair involved her convincing me how good it looked. But considering the state I was in, it was probably exactly what I needed. I didn't have any more days to take off of work. I would be forced to face the world with my short, nappy hair.

"There is nothing wrong with short, nappy hair. Hair is hair," she had said. "Straight is beautiful, curly is beautiful, nappy is beautiful. If you don't believe that, how will anyone else?"

Logically, what she said made sense. I just didn't believe it. If our nappy hair was so beautiful, why did we spend our lives trying to hide it? Even as she was saying this I was thinking back to when I was six years old sitting in my grandmother's hot kitchen getting my hair straightened with a hot comb. If my nappy hair was so beautiful, why did I have to spend two hours using fire to straighten it? And what was worse, was that after spending all that time getting my neck and ears burned by a hot comb, I was no longer allowed to go outside and play with my friends for fear I would 'sweat it out'. Forget summer swim camps. I couldn't get my hair wet for fear my hair would revert back to its natural nappy state. As far as I could see, there was no beauty in this hair. But I would sure pretend there was.

Carnece tried to convince me to wear a wig to my first day back at work for an easier transition. She even had a couple in her car that I could try on. But they just didn't look right on me. Probably because one had a streak of hot pink and the other had a streak of purple. Not exactly my style.

I'd never had Wash N Go hair. All my life, doing my hair was a process that required me clearing two days off of my schedule. So despite my hatred of my new hair, I kind of loved being able to just hop out of the shower, rub in a little oil and gel, and head out. It was kind of freeing. No, I didn't love the style, but I did love the freedom.

I dreaded the looks I would get with my hair like this. I especially dreaded what Trent would say. I hated that guy. He always had something to say about everything. And usually, whatever he had to say was offensive and laced with profanity.

The morning began without even a word from him. Just a look. A look I didn't quite understand. He just stared at me for several seconds from his desk that was unfortunately just inches away from mine. I decided to make a preemptive strike.

"Yes, I changed my hair," I said slamming down my bag and staring at him. "And I happen to like it." Okay, that was a bit of a lie, but he didn't need to know that. "This is the way my hair grows out of my head and this is the way I'm going to wear it."

Trent still didn't say anything. After a few more seconds of staring he said, "That..." He didn't finish his thought. He kind of just trailed off and kept staring at me. I knew what he was thinking. He probably wanted to say something racist and offensive like how I looked like a slave or something. Once I caught him talking about how he just wasn't attracted to black girls. I walked in the break room just as he was telling Ray how he didn't understand how anyone could find a black woman attractive.

"What? What are you trying to say?" I asked standing my ground. I was not going to let him intimidate me.

He shook his head as if trying to wake himself up. "Nothing. Didn't say anything." Then he took out his wallet, pulled out a dollar, and stuffed it into a jar sitting on his desk.

For the past three months, he had been constantly stuffing money into an old jelly jar on his desk. I had no idea why and before today I had never even cared to ask. But given that he just stared at me before dropping money into it, I had to admit that I was a little curious.

Just when I was about to ask what was going on with the jar and the cash, Sharon, the company accountant, walked by and said, "Welcome to the club."

"What club?" I asked.

Pointing to her head she said, "Natural hair. You're going to love it."

Honestly, I had never noticed that she was natural. But looking at it now, I could see that she had an adorable afro puff sitting at the top of her head. I had to admit, I was a little jealous of it. If my hair was long enough to poof like that I think I would like it a whole lot more. But right now I felt I looked like a boy. I had to make sure I wore something extremely feminine to counteract the effect of my lack of hair.

"Thanks," I said to Sharon as she kept walking toward accounting.

The momentary confidence I felt from Sharon's comment soon evaporated as Eliza came over to my desk. Eliza was an eighteen year old intern who had just graduated high school and was trying to get some experience in marketing before going off to college. I was less than ten years older than her, but the way she spoke like a walking text message made me feel like we were in completely different generations. "OMG! I knew you were sick, but I didn't know it was that bad. SMH. You should have told someone," she said.

"Told someone what?" I asked.

"About the cancer. It was cancer right?"

I touched my hair self-consciously.

"You dumb ass," Trent said out of the blue. "She's been gone less than a week. You really think chemo works that fast?" Trent took a quarter out of his pocket and dropped it into the jar before saying, "Why don't you go turn on some Justin Bieber and let the adults get some work done, okay?"

"You see, this is why no one likes you," Eliza said.

"Are you still talking? Are you really still talking? Mahogany, is there blood dripping out of my ears?" Trent asked touching the sides of his face dramatically. "Cause I'm pretty sure the sound of idiot teenagers makes my ears bleed."

Eliza rolled her eyes and stormed away.

"A little harsh there, Trent," I said after she had gone.

He shrugged. "Whatever. I hate that kid. She makes me want to get a vasectomy for my 30th birthday." He cleared his throat and said, "Your hair looks good like that. She's a moron. Trust me. Last week she was confused at how a pencil sharpener worked."

"Still, she's just a kid," I said. "You could have found a nicer way to say it."

Trent looked straight ahead. I could tell there were some things going on in his head. Thankfully, he didn't share. Inside his psycho brain was probably one scary place. Once again, he took a dollar out of his wallet and stuffed it in his jar.

"What is it with you and that jar?" I asked trying to count the money in it. There had to be almost twenty dollars.

Trent grabbed it and put it in his desk. "You don't want to know," he said after slamming the drawer shut.

"If I didn't want to know, I wouldn't have asked."

Instead of responding, he stood up and walked away. What a jerk.

~~~

There are a couple of things you should probably know about the social media firm where I work. It is run by my boss Mr. George who refuses to admit that he is going bald and about to turn 60. Therefore he does everything in his power to seem hip and cool which includes growing his hair to his shoulders and running his company as if it was a candy factory. A few months ago, he decided that desks were too conventional and made everyone get rid of them and go to bean bags. He also instituted a companywide weekly fitness regime which really only included putting on yoga pants and breathing deeply. I think I put up with all the weird stuff because the pay was great and the job was really flexible. But the one thing I couldn't stand was the bathroom thing. Since Mr. George believed that men and women were created equal, he felt we should all use the same bathroom. Therefore, we had one bathroom with three stalls inside for all forty-two people in the company to use. Because of this, I usually waited until lunch to go to the bathroom, but today I couldn't wait. After the cancer comment from Eliza I needed somewhere to go shed a few tears. And I refused to cry in front of my workmates.

I waited until it was clear and then slipped into our stupid unisex bathroom.

It only took a quick look at my horrible hair before the tears started. What had I done? What was I doing? I had cut Vinny and my hair out of my life. Maybe I would go wig shopping with Carnece after work.

As I heard the door swing open, I tried to wipe away tears and get myself together.

"Oh, sorry," Trent said from the door.

Great, I thought. All I needed was for him to go around telling everyone in the office how I was blubbering in the bathroom.

"I'll just go," he said backing out of the bathroom.

The fact that Trent saw me like this made me cry even more.

"Uh, you don't want to go in there," I heard Trent say from outside. Great. This was his chance.

"Why not?"

"It needs to air out. I had bad sushi and, uh, what I just did in there was not a pretty sight," he added.

Was he covering for me? Why?

Ten minutes later when I was finally able to stop crying, I stepped outside the bathroom to find Trent still standing there.

I cleared my throat and said, "Thanks."

He shrugged and said, "Never happened."

Chapter 5: TWA

TWA: Teenie Weenie Afro. Yeah, this is also pretty self-explanatory. It's an afro that's kind of small, maybe no more than three inches or so even fully picked out.

~~~

Hair tip #4: By using a moisture and gel, you may be able to add adorable curls to your TWA. Take one small section of hair at a time, add a moisturizer and then twist the hair around your finger with the gel. It does not need to be as perfectly defined as finger coils.

~~~

*L*et's face it. My big hair chop was an unconscious attempt to symbolize cutting Vinny out of my life. It kind of made sense. But, unfortunately, my conscious mind didn't completely agree with my unconscious mind. I hated my hair. And when you hate your hair, it's kind of hard to like anything else about yourself.

I think I might have been able to deal with my natural hair a little better if it was longer. I'd have more confidence if I had a huge sweeping afro like Angela Davis or something. But as it was, all I had was a TWA, a Teenie Weenie Afro. It took all of my effort to look confident and pretend like I loved my hair when most days all I wanted to do was crawl into a corner and cry. No amount of colorful flowers in my hair or jewelry could change the fact that I felt extremely ugly and unattractive, especially to the opposite sex.

I just wanted my hair to grow, and quickly. Like the nerd I am, I started doing research to figure out what I could do to help my hair grow faster. There had to be some kind of vitamin I could take or a special elixir to massage into my scalp.

From my research, I learned that human hair grows an average of six inches per year. The only way to increase that was to have a healthy protein rich diet and take vitamin supplements. This might increase the growth rate to seven or eight inches per year.

Somehow I thought chopping off all of my hair or breaking up with my boyfriend of seven years would be the hardest thing I'd have to encounter for a while, but I was sadly mistaken. The hardest thing would be telling my parents that I had cut off said hair and broken up with said boyfriend.

"Sweetheart, it's your life," my dad said leaning against the wall of my apartment sipping a glass of merlot. I had inherited my attachment to red wine from him. My mother was more of a gin and tonic kind of girl. "But do you really want to break up with him over something like this. I mean marriage isn't all it's cracked up to be. Look at your mother and me."

"Amen to that!" my mother said from the computer screen. She was on one of her yearly shopping trips in New York and thus had to join the conversation through Skype. "And please, for the love of God, let me send you some cash so you can get that hair fixed. I think my stylist will still be able to sew in a nice weave."

"I don't want a weave. I like my hair just the way it is." Okay, I was back to the same old lie once again, but I was not about to admit that I thought my hair was a mistake to my parents. They would just use that as a sign of weakness and then somehow convince me to get back together with Vinny.

"Well, I don't understand what made you think he was going to propose in the first place," my dad said pouring himself another glass.

"Really? You don't understand? Well, let's see, we've been together for seven years and he had lunch with you three weeks ago."

"Honey, I'm a mortgage broker. We were just working on his loan." His calm demeanor and perfectly tailored suit was really starting to piss me off for some reason. I suddenly felt like I was presenting my case before Congress or something.

"Of course, it seems obvious now, but at the time -"

"Well, you're never going to get him back with your hair like that, Mahogany," my mother said interrupting me. "You have to do something."

"Who the hell says I want him back?"

My mother and father rolled their eyes simultaneously. For two people who hated each other so much, they sure did agree when it came to my life.

After my dad left and my mother signed off, I went back to my hair books. I took out a ruler and tried to measure my hair. I was going to test the half inch a month statistic for the next month. I really wanted to see how much my hair would grow. If it really did grow half an inch or more, all hope was not lost. I could make a goal of how long I wanted it to be in a year. I would follow a strict hair growing diet if I had to. This was the new me. A new life, a new journey, and my key to getting over Vinyay Gupta.

Chapter 6: Sister Locks

Sisterlocks: Tiny uniform locks that are the result of a precision parting grid, and the use a specialized tool used to place the hair into its locking formation.

~~~

Hair tip #5: Jealousy ain't cute. There is no need to be jealous of hair styles that your hair just can't do. Learn your hair texture and do styles that compliment it and you.

~~~

*T*hough I was slowly getting used to my new hair, I still wasn't completely comfortable. Yes, I went to work every day, but that was about it. I didn't go hang out with my girls on the weekends like I used to. I went to work because I had to pay the bills. Going clubbing wasn't a necessity, so I didn't do it. I just didn't feel cute enough to get into my tiny little outfits and party. Instead, I spent all my spare time in my apartment watching YouTube videos about natural hair care trying to find the right combination of things to do with my hair in order to make me love it.

After a month and a half of this, I think my friends started to worry.

"Mahogany Brown, you better open up this door before I knock it down," Marin said while banging on my front door. I wasn't in the mood for Marin. I would have hidden under the bed or something, but I knew she wasn't kidding about the knocking down the door thing. I didn't need one of my neighbors calling the police or something. Going down to the station to bail my sister-in-law out of jail was not what I considered a fun Sunday afternoon.

"I'm coming!" I yelled as I made my way to the front door. Before opening, I slapped on a silk scarf. I was not in the mood to talk hair. Especially with Marin. Her hair was amazing. She had these beautiful sisterlocks that reached down to the middle of her back. I had often admired her hair. But I was too chicken to take the step into dreadlocks. They were so permanent. What if I changed my mind after a year or something? I'd have to cut them all off and start over. What if Vinny didn't like them? Vinny. Well, I guess I didn't really have to worry about what he would or wouldn't like any more.

"What are you doing here, Marin?" I asked as I opened the door. Considering she and my brother lived all the way in Philadelphia, it wasn't like her showing up at my door was a regular occurrence. It wasn't that I didn't like my sister-in-law. She was awesome. I loved her and I totally understand why my brother married her the same day they met. She had one of those big personalities that you couldn't help but love. She could start talking to a complete stranger on the bus and ten minutes later have a new best friend. I think she had about three thousand and twenty eight best friends.

"Is that how you greet me? I haven't seen you in two months. Get over here and give your big sister a hug." She wrapped her arms around me and hugged me tight. For a little thing she sure had a strong grip. Marin walked in and went straight to the kitchen. She reached in my cabinet and pulled out my tea kettle. In her mind, there was no problem that couldn't be fixed with hot tea, warm milk, or a cold ginger beer. So she always had one of the three with her at all times.

Once the tea was made, she set it down on the coffee table and said, "Okay, tell me what's going on."

I wasn't a big fan of tea, but I took a sip anyway just to delay having to speak. "Nothing. I'm fine," I said finally.

"No you're not. No one is fine right after breaking up a relationship as long as yours and Vinny's."

I shrugged. "Maybe I'm not fine, but I'm getting there."

"Mahogany, you don't have to *get there* alone," she said. "You have family, you have friends. Don't shut people out."

I closed my eyes tightly to seal in tears. She was right. I had been blocking people out. "You know what I think the problem is?" I said with my eyes still closed. "Everyone I know reminds me of him. Every time I see someone, I think about the first time I introduced them to Vinny."

Marin nodded. "I understand that. The first time I met him was a week after I married your brother. I knew then and there he wasn't the one for you."

Opening my eyes I said, "What do you mean?"

Marin took a sip of tea. "It was just a feeling. That's why I didn't say anything. But now I know that first instinct was right."

"What first instinct? What did you think of him? Why didn't you tell me?"

"I learned a long time ago that you don't get involved in other people's love lives. Especially women. No offense, but women can be so stupid and stubborn sometimes."

"Um, Marin, you're a woman, too."

"Which is why I know? Duh?" She stood up and grabbed her purse which she had left by the door. "We need to change the energy in this room. The negativity is downright stifling." She lit an incense candle and started waving it around the room. Was that her nice way of saying my house stunk?

"Wait a minute, Marin. Don't try to change the subject. What did you see in Vinny the first time you met him?"

Marin sat back down on the couch and said, "The first time I met him, I noticed his eyes when you hugged John. He was jealous. He was jealous of how close you two were. What kind of a man gets jealous of his girlfriend's brother? Jealousy ain't cute. I just knew I didn't like him."

"Huh, I didn't know you felt that way. Why didn't you ever tell me?"

"I could have been wrong. I know, I know. It doesn't happen often. I think the last time I was wrong it was around 1998."

I pushed her in the shoulder.

"Anyway," she said after we laughed a little. "Add that jealous streak to the fact that you've never met his family in seven years, well, I knew it wasn't going to work."

"Yeah, that was a red flag I refused to salute."

"I mean, his sister is in Canada. That's not that far. One quick two hour flight would have fixed it. And haven't either of you heard of Skype? I'm sure they have computers in India. I know every time I try to get mine fixed I'm talking to someone from there."

"Marin, that's not nice."

She shrugged and went back to spreading her incense smoke all over my house. "So what are you going to do?" she asked.

"What do you mean? What am I supposed to do? It's over. I wanted a husband not a roommate. There's nothing for me to do."

"Oh, no, I know it's over. I mean what is your catharsis?"

"Catharsis?"

"Yes, catharsis. You have to do something big that symbolically represents the end of your relationship. Usually, I have a system. Each month I was with a guy represents the level of catharsis I need. For example, I dated this guy Mikhail for almost two years and when we broke up, I went sky diving."

I shivered at the thought. I was afraid of heights.

"But given that you were with Vinny for almost seven years, you'd need to jump out of a space shuttle to make up for that."

I rubbed my hand over the scarf hiding my short hair. "I think I already had my catharsis," I said as I slowly pulled it off.

Marin screamed and jumped on the couch. Not quite the reaction I was expecting.

"This is so exciting," she said clapping her hands and squealing like a child. "I love it. I love it. I love it!"

"Marin, calm down. What's to love about it? It's short, nappy and ugly."

Suddenly solemn, she stopped jumping and sat down again. "Mahogany, don't you ever let me hear you say something like that about our hair again."

"*Our* hair? *Our* hair doesn't look like this. Your hair is long and beautiful. It's just mine that sucks."

"You see this is what is wrong with our society. People associate beauty with long hair. I don't understand why those are so often correlated." She stood up and started pacing my living room as if she was going to give a sermon. "I'll tell you where the problem starts. It starts when we're little girls and we are constantly told through the images we see in the media that long, straight, blond hair is what is pretty. Kinky or curly hair is ugly. Do they sell Barbie dolls with afros? And when was the last time a black woman was the leading lady of a romance movie."

"Halle Berry," I volunteered.

"She doesn't count. She's half black and full horrible actress."

"What does her acting ability have to do with it?"

"Basically, what society says is that white skin and straight hair is attractive. Black women are only attractive if they are as close to white as possible."

"Marin, calm down."

"I'm sorry. I will not calm down. This is a pet peeve of mine. Do you know that black women are the least often married." She froze and looked at me. "Sorry."

I took a deep breath to hold in the tears. "Deep down I know that's why he doesn't want to marry me. He's ashamed of my race."

Marin took my hands in hers and sat next to me. "Which is exactly why I'm so happy about your hair," she said. "It's about time you embraced your blackness and started to love yourself for your innate beauty. Love yourself for exactly who you are."

Yeah, I still didn't know what she meant. What did my hair have to do with her happiness?

"In fact," she added as she dropped my hands and started looking around. "I'm going to take this step with you." She picked up a pair of scissors and before I could stop her started chopping off her beautiful sisterlocks.

"What are you doing? Are you crazy?"

"What? It's just hair. It will grow back. That's its only job. To grow."

"But what will John say?"

She looked at me strangely. "Why in the world would he care what I do with my hair? It's *my* hair not his." She went back to cutting. "This is perfect. Trust me. These dreads are getting long. Summer is coming. I don't want to be hot, fat and pregnant and have to deal with all this hair."

"Wait. Pregnant?"

She turned and smiled at me. "You're going to be an aunt."

I screamed and hugged her. At least one of us would be phenomenally happy.

Chapter 7: Set back

Set Back: During the natural hair journey you may suffer a setback due to heat damage, color damage, or just plain frustration which causes you to do another big chop. It happens to almost everyone.

~~~

Hair tip #6: If you have a setback, don't get discouraged. Just start the journey again. Growing natural hair isn't a race; it's a life style change.

~~~

My setback came on a Tuesday in May. My hair was in that in between stage where it was too long for a wash n go, but too short to pull back into a poof. It had also started behaving badly. It felt dry, knotty and downright unattractive. I felt like there was nothing I could do with it. For work that day I picked it out and put a flower in it. It was enough to get me through the day. But by the time I got home, I literally wanted to shave my head. Instead, I took out the scissors and a bottle of wine. I turned on some Otis Redding and started drinking my feelings.

Merlot and Otis Redding were two things I had inherited from my father. I could always tell when he had had a bad day because he would easily go through a bottle of red and four or five Otis Redding CD's. He told me it was something he had learned from *his* father. Though in those days it was albums. Personally, I preferred my Otis playlist on my iPod. I didn't have to worry about switching CDs or dusting off records. It was three straight hours of soul-drenching rhythm and blues.

I danced around my apartment with my glass of wine in one hand and a pair of scissors in the other wondering when I was going to make the first snip. It had to be done. My hair at this length was too hard to handle and at the rate it was growing, it would be months before it got to a length that I wanted.

Halfway through a bottle of wine and while belting out the lyrics to *Try a Little Tenderness* I heard the doorbell ring.

"What are you doing here?" I asked Vinny who was standing in my doorway holding a cardboard box. It had been well over two months since I had seen him.

"I was clearing out my apartment and I found some of your stuff," he said referring to the box. "Are you okay? Why are you playing Otis? What happened?"

I smiled a little. He remembered. He remembered how I played Otis Redding whenever I was depressed. But of course, after seven years he *should* remember something like that.

I wasn't thinking clearly though. It could have been the wine, or it could have been the fact that I hadn't gotten laid since two weeks before we had broken up, but

I suddenly wanted him. I wanted him so bad. Maybe it wasn't him exactly that I wanted. Maybe I just wanted to feel loved and desired. In any case, I invited him in.

"You want a drink?" I asked after Vinny had set down the box on my dining room table.

"Yeah sure."

I went to the fridge and pulled out a bottle of his favorite beer that I hadn't gotten rid of yet. After I handed it to him, I topped off my wine glass. Vinny sat on my couch and put his feet up on my coffee table. I used to hate when he did that, but tonight I didn't mind. I just liked that he was there. I missed him. I missed us. *Try a Little Tenderness* ended and the next song started *I've Been Loving You Too Long*. The lyrics were so true. I'd loved Vinny for so long. Why stop now?

After chugging my glass of wine, I sat down next to him on the couch and put my head on his chest.

"Maggie, what's wrong?"

I leaned up and looked into his eyes. "I just miss you," I said.

"Oh, Maggie," he whispered against my lips. "I miss you too." When he kissed me, it was like no time had passed. It was just as the way things had always been. In fact, it was better. After being together for so long, our sex life could sometimes slip into a routine. But tonight was different. Probably because it had been almost three months since we had touched each other.

Vinny was slow and considerate as he made love to me not leaving even an inch of my body undiscovered. I was in ecstasy. That was until the wine wore off and I realized what I had done.

Leslie DuBois

I stared at Vinny's naked body tangled up in my bed sheets. What kind of a person was I? We didn't even have a conversation before I practically jumped his bones. What the hell was wrong with me?

Vinny groaned and rolled over as if he was about to wake up. I didn't feel like talking to him. Not yet. I had to figure out what I was doing and why. I slipped out of bed and went to the kitchen to put on a pot of coffee. The clock said four thirty. That was early even for me. I sat at my dining room table for nearly two hours. After all that time, I still wasn't sure what I was doing. How could I let Vinny back into my life? Nothing had changed. Had it?

"Why are you up so early?" Vinny said coming out of the bedroom scratching his naked belly. "It's Saturday."

"You know me. I like to get an early start," I got up and walked to the kitchen while awkwardly trying to avoid eye contact with him.

"So we didn't really talk much last night," he said sitting down at the table. "Which, honestly, was quite all right with me. But we should probably talk now. Can I get a cup of coffee?"

Wordlessly, I poured the last bit of the pot into a cup and then placed it in front of him. Vinny reached out and touched my hair. "What is up with your hair?"

"What do you mean?"

"What did you do to it? It never looked that way before."

I sighed. I didn't feel like going into it. He wouldn't understand. Suddenly I wished I had the kind of relationship with Vinny that Marin had with my brother.

50

She didn't even consider what John would think when she cut her hair. As she said, it was *her* hair not his. But with Vinny, it was different. I suddenly realized that Vinny was often concerned with the way I looked. Maybe a little too concerned.

"What did you want to talk about, Vinny?" I asked sitting across from him.

"About us," he said before taking a sip.

"There is no us." I didn't even know I was going to say that. It just came out.

Vinny set down his cup and stared at me. "What do you mean? What about last night?"

"Last night..." I sighed. "I was lonely and depressed and I needed someone."

"And you got me. You need me and you have me. Forever."

"Really, Vinny? Forever? How am I supposed to know I have you forever?"

"Is this about getting married again? God, Maggie, what is with you? Why is marriage so important? Why can't things be the way they've always been?"

That was a good question. He had a right to an answer to it. And I finally had a response.

"Because I'm not the same as I've always been, okay? I've changed and I need more. I need more than what you can give me."

"Well, you seemed to enjoy what I gave you last night," he said with a smirk. You have to understand something about Vinyay Gupta. He wasn't trying to be hurtful when he said that. He honestly thought he was being funny. Like everything was one big joke. He would probably go write that down so he could share it with his roommate later.

I stormed off to my bedroom and slammed the door. Then I opened it again and tossed out his clothing. He could find his way out by himself. As for me, I turned on some more Otis Redding and curled up under the sheets.

I realized this was a major setback, but I was going to get through. I had to. There was no way I was getting back together with Vinyay Gupta.

Chapter 9: Locked

Locks: Often called dreadlocks. Twisted, matted, ropes of hair.

~~~

Hair tip #7: Dreadlocks are a big commitment but not as big as you think. There are several YouTube videos showing how people have unlocked their hair and kept their length. It is a process that takes several days, but it can be done. If you're not sure you are ready for locks, try twists that you take out and redo every month. Your hair won't lock, but you'll still have a similar look. Plus twists are a great protective style meaning it protects your hair from breaking off unnecessarily.

~~~

Most mornings I made my own coffee at home. Life was expensive and I was too cheap to waste five bucks a day on a cup of whipped cream with a side of caffeine. This morning was different, however. I was in such a good mood I felt I needed to treat myself. I also thought I needed some sort of reward for going a full three weeks without contacting Vinny after my setback.

I was rocking my twist out so my hair looked funky and fresh. All I had to do was whip on my skinny jeans, boots, and a cream knit sweater. My flair trench finished off the look and I have to say that look was fierce. There's something about when your hair does exactly what it's supposed to do that puts you in a good mood.

Standing in line at the Bean Machine a head of pristine dreadlocks caught my eye. That's another side effect of going natural that I noticed. I am constantly looking at other people's hairstyles searching for ideas or tips. This time my staring kind of got me in trouble. The gorgeous dreadlocks happened to belong to the head of an equally gorgeous man who completely caught me checking him out. I turned away embarrassed. But then I was even more embarrassed when I realized that he worked at the Bean Machine and had switched places with a coworker so that he could take my order.

"Can I help you?" he asked.

I was momentarily dumbstruck as I visually drunk him all in. His skin was like liquid dark chocolate and his voice like deep sweet wine. All in all, he was just plain tasty.

"I think I'll have a coffee," I said, my voice suddenly getting two pitches higher.

He smiled and I almost stopped breathing. "Well, I think you've come to the right place," he said. Suddenly I couldn't stop staring at his lips. They were thick and luscious and I wondered if they tasted like fudge. "So, what kind of coffee would you like?"

"Uh...." Yeah, I couldn't think straight anymore. What did he mean? Coffee was coffee. I didn't really care what I was about to drink as long as he was going to hand it to me.

"Don't worry. I'll fix you something sweet," he said with a wink. He left the register and started throwing things together. I didn't really even pay attention to what he was putting into the cup. I was just looking at him. His tight, neat dreads fell to the middle of his back. How long did it take him to grow his hair that long? I wondered if I should get dreads.

"Here you go," he said a few minutes later.

"What is it?"

"All you need to know is written on the cup," he winked again then went back to helping more customers.

I looked at the cup. Apparently all I needed to know was:

Jaames
555-1312

~~~

My good day had gotten so much better with my trip to the coffee shop. I was going on a date. A date with a gorgeous man. It would be my first date since Vinny. My stomach tightened. I had been with Vinny for the better part of a decade. Did I even know how to date anymore?

And now I was starting to panic. I dreaded calling that number written on the cup. What was I supposed to say?

"You all right?" Trent asked as he stepped on to the elevator.

"Yes, fine. Why?"

He looked around and then back at me. "You're standing in the elevator staring at a cup. The doors have opened and closed three times.

"Really? Oh, right." I stepped to the side and let Trent have his space in the elevator. No one else was around. With our laid back company, none of the other employees came in until 9:30 or 10. Trent and I were apparently morning people. We were often at the office well before eight. We stayed out of each other's way though. Either he would go to the break room and read the paper or I would head to the rooftop garden and read some paper work.

Trent pressed the eighth floor button then did what I call the awkward elevator stare. You know when you just stare at the numbers in front of you watching them light up as if you need the practice counting.

Standing two feet away from a guy I hate while watching little numbers light up was precisely when my good day went oh so wrong.

Suddenly, the elevator stopped. It just completely stopped moving. I was stuck on an elevator with Trent Bishop.

The first thing that went through my mind was that I wouldn't be able to go on a date with James now. I would never know what it would feel like to be wrapped in his warm chocolate embrace. Yeah, a little dramatic, I know.

I had no idea what was going on in Trent's mind. Of course, that was nothing new. Trent closed his eyes and took a deep breath. Then he opened up his wallet and took out a dollar. Holding it up, he said, "Take this please."

I looked around. "Are you talking to me?" Stupid question yes I know since we were the only ones in the elevator. I just didn't understand why he was handing me a dollar. Did he expect me to dance for him or something?

"Yes, you. Will you take it please and put it in my jar when we get out of here?"

"I'll take it on one condition," I said, holding my hand above the dollar.

"Yeah, fine, anything."

"You have to tell me what's up with the whole jar thing."

Still holding the dollar in the air, he kept staring at the light up numbers as if willing them to start moving again. He stuffed the dollar in his pocket, opened up that little door with the emergency phone in it and started pushing buttons. Then he started pushing the alarm expecting someone to contact us and tell us help was on the way. When they didn't, he sighed and said, "Fine." He took the dollar out again. I grabbed it and dropped it in my purse just as he loosened his tie and sat on the floor.

"I used to be a pretty awful person," he began.

"You mean, worse than you are now?"

He glared at me. "Do you want to know about the jar or not?"

"Sorry. Continue." I set down my purse and sat down across from him.

"I got accustomed to watching bad music, bad movies and playing violent and offensive video games."

"Like what?" I asked. I don't know why I asked that. Oh who am I kidding? Yes, I do.

"Do you know the game Blood Kill?"

"Yep. My boyfriend...I mean, my ex-boyfriend created some of the graphics for that game." It was his first project. He actually started it while he was still in college. The game was so bloody, violent, and foul that it had been attacked by several community decency groups which sent sales through the roof.

"Anyway," he continued. "Over the years I noticed that my manner of speech started to imitate the games and movies that I was so addicted to. Normally, that wouldn't be a problem, but eight months ago, at my grandmother's birthday I had a little bit of an awakening."

"What do you mean?"

"I slipped and cursed out my eight year old cousin for spilling coleslaw on my pants. It was embarrassing. The kid cried, my aunt cried, my grandmother cried. A week later, my family actually had an intervention with me and made me swear...well, promise to clean up my...potty-mouth. I tried to stop on my own, but it was nearly impossible when all I did was watch movies and play games with that kind of language. So I stopped watching the movies and games. I got a little better but I still found that I slipped a lot. So I came up with the jar. Different words have different dollar values. If I even think a bad word, I have to put money in the far. If I actually say it, I have to pay it double."

I thought about the jar on his desk. It was almost always nearly full by the end of the day. Wow, that boy had a lot of dirty thoughts. But it was kind of admirable of him that he was trying to change.

"So what do you use the money for?"

He shrugged.

"Cause that's a lot of money."

"Yeah, I know."

"I'm sure you could buy a car or something by now."

"Yeah, I know."

"And I'm not talking a crappy used car. I think you could buy a Mercedes or something with all the money that has been in that jar."

"Okay, I get it," he said glaring at me again. I don't think I had ever actually met his glare before. It was the first time I noticed his electric blue eyes. I felt that electricity all through me. I turned away and stared at my coffee cup again.

"So what's so special about that coffee?" he asked a few moments later.

Normally, this is way too much conversation for Trent and me. But since we were stuck in an elevator and had nothing else to do but talk, I decided to share.

I turned the cup around to show off the phone number. "I met a guy this morning."

He nodded. "Must be love," he said sarcastically. "You should go ahead and marry him. Today. Why wait?"

"What are you talking about? I just met him this morning?"

"So what? Given that half of all marriages end in divorce, I say you have about a 50/50 shot at a successful marriage no matter what. Why not just marry a random person?"

I started to dispute him until I realized he was kind of right. My parents dated for ten years before they got married and were divorced less than three years later. On the other hand John married Marin the day they met. Three years later they were happier than ever.

Trent folded his jacket into a pillow and placed it behind his head before leaning back and closing his eyes. I guessed the conversation was over. It was our first real conversation in the whole year and a half we had worked together. I couldn't help but notice the undertone of bitterness in his voice when he talked about marriage. I wondered if he spoke from experience. Maybe he was going through a divorce and that was why he was so bitter.

"By the way," he said a few minutes later with his eyes still closed. "Anyone who spells James with two a's is going to be a complete prick." Trent stuck his hand in his pocket and pulled out a quarter.

I looked at my coffee cup again. Yeah, Jaames with two As. Now that I thought about it, who in the world would spell James with two 'A's?

"Why don't you call him?" Trent asked.

"What, now?"

He shrugged. "Got anything better else to do?"

He was right, of course. I didn't have anything else to do. I took out my phone. "No bars," I said noticing the lack of reception. James with two 'A's would have to wait.

Chapter 10: Flat Twists

Flat Twists: Twists of hair against the scalp. They can kind of resemble corn rows.

~~~

Hair tip #8: Flat twists are another great protective style. They look fabulous on their own, plus after you wear them for a few days, you can undo them into a nice twist out style.

~~~

Hair tip #9: The curl pattern of African American hair prevents the natural oils from the scalp from traveling all the way to the ends of the hair. That is why black people do not need to wash their hair as often. That is also why they have to add oils to it. Washing the hair can strip the hair of the oils it needs to keep from breaking. Try a co-wash in between regular washings in order to keep as much oil and moisture in the hair as possible. A co-wash means washing your hair with conditioner instead of shampoo.

~~~

W hy are you flipping out?" Carnece asked a month later as she sectioned my hair.

"Why? *Why,* you ask? I haven't been on a first date in seven years. I don't even think I know how to do it anymore. I mean, what do you do? Who pays? Is it just dinner? Is there dancing later? What if he wants to go back to my place?"

"Why are you asking me all this? You're the one who called James with two A's. What did *he* say?" Carnece asked. She started adding a crème moisturizer and working it into the sections of hair.

"He said we were going for coffee and then going to listen to a jazz combo."

"Well then you're going for coffee and then to listen to a jazz combo," she said.

"You make it seem so simple."

"And you make it seem so complicated."

She had a point there. Maybe it was that simple. I was only going to go sit and talk with a man who I found very attractive. We would just get to know each other over coffee and jazz music. But that right there was intimidating enough. I didn't want to have to get to know someone new. I wanted someone who I was comfortable with. Someone I already knew.

I sat in silence as Carnece flat twisted my hair. That was the wrong attitude. Vinny was my past. Maybe Jaames was my future. But I'd never know if I didn't give this dating thing a try.

~~~

Flat Twists

We met at the coffee shop where he worked. According to Carnece, she never lets a man pick her up on the first date. She doesn't want a guy to know where she lives until she's sure he's not a psycho. Even that backfires though. She says sometimes the psycho part of a man doesn't come out until date five or six and then you just have to move.

"You look great," Jaames said, giving me a hug. "I'm so happy you called me."

"You too. Me too. I mean..." I took a deep breath and started over. "You look great too. And I'm happy I called as well. I'm sorry it took me almost a month."

Smiling he said, "Have a seat and I'll go grab us a couple of coffees."

I watched him walk away staring at the muscles in his butt flex under his jeans. I was always a girl into butts. I don't know why. Mostly I liked to just admire them. I couldn't do much more, especially considering that Vinny had the flattest butt of all time. I wondered what it would be like to grab Jaames' butt during the throes of passion. I flushed a little. How was I already thinking about sleeping with him? Was it even common to have sex on the first date or would he think I was a slut?

"So how long have you worked here?" I asked when he came back trying to get my mind off of sex and on to mundane conversation.

He rolled up the sleeves on his crisp lavender shirt and leaned back in his chair. "I've worked here off and on since it opened. It's my brother's shop. I just come in once in a while to help him out."

"Well, you make great coffee," I said, taking a sip of the whip cream topped latte he had set in front of me.

"Thanks. But I wouldn't call it my calling or anything. It's just something I do to help him out. I'm going to show you what I really do later tonight."

My eyes expanded. What the hell was he talking about? Could he somehow tell that I wanted to have sex with him? Was I that transparent? If that was the case, he could also probably tell that I hadn't gotten any in over three months. Oh God, how embarrassing.

"Oh no, that's not what I mean," he said almost spilling his coffee. "I'm a musician. The jazz combo we're going to see is mine. The Jaames Monroe Trio."

"Oh, okay." Now I felt stupid for even thinking about it.

"So what about you? What do you do?"

I smiled nervously. I always felt silly telling people what I did for a living. I basically surfed the internet all day. It's hard to believe there was even a market for what I did, but we had lots of business.

"I work for a social media firm called By George," I said.

"So what does that mean?" he asked.

"It means I handle the social media accounts of people that are too busy to do it themselves."

"So you're behind people's Facebook, blogs, and twitter."

I nodded. "Not only that, but Google+, pinterest, tumblr, and any other social media platforms that pop up overnight."

"Wow, that actually sounds like a lot of work."

I smiled appreciatively. Finally, someone who understood what I did on a regular basis. Vinny always thought I spent my day just playing on the internet. Which was rather ironic since he literally played video games all day and called it research.

"It is a lot of work actually. For our more popular clients I could be doing more than a hundred tweets and posts a day. Thankfully, I can schedule a lot of them in advance and have a few hours of freedom during the day once in a while. But even during my free time I have to do research into new avenues of reaching a fan base."

"So who are some of your more famous clients?"

"I can't really say. I mean, it wouldn't be good for business for fans to know that their favorite celebrities aren't the ones writing the Facebook posts they're so excited to read."

He nodded. I liked talking to him. He understood what I did and even appreciated it.

"What about me?" he asked.

"Excuse me?"

"Could you do the social media for my jazz combo?"

"Yeah, I think I could. What do you have so far?" I reached into my purse and pulled out my iPhone. "What's your twitter handle?"

"Uh, I don't have one."

"Okay, what about your Facebook page?"

He shook his head.

"Surely you have a website."

"Sort of."

James with two 'A's then proceeded to direct me to one of those free websites where there was a picture of his band along with a few listings of concert dates. It hadn't even been updated in over two months.

"Yeah, you definitely need my help."

~~~

"Can you do me a little favor?" I asked Trent the next day at work.

He stared at me as if he didn't know how to respond. We weren't exactly the kind of workmates that did favors for one another. I mean we rarely spoke on a regular basis. But I could tell I was more of his friend than anyone else in the building. We had been stuck in an elevator together for more than an hour and we didn't kill each other. I don't think he would have been able to accomplish that with anyone else.

"I need you to look at some work I did last night and give me your opinion," I said when he didn't respond.

It was a good thirty minutes before anyone else would even arrive so it wasn't like he had pressing work to do.

"Okay," he said simply.

I scooted over to his desk and typed in the address for the website I had created for Jaames' band. Trent was the website expert. He was behind all the gorgeous websites most of our clients had. I had no idea how he had time to maintain all of them, but he did. I knew it would be too expensive for Jaames to hire Trent's services so I decided to give it a try myself.

After navigating around the website for a few moments, Trent cleared his throat and said, "It's nice."

"I know it's nothing compared to what you can do, but I tried."

He cleared his throat again like it was difficult to pay me a compliment. "No, it's really good. I can't believe you did this in one night."

"To be fair, I used a template, but I did have to do some hard coding. I could use some tips to make it better if you have any."

"Is that him?" Trent asked pointing to one of the members of the band.

"Who?"

"James with two 'A's."

"No, him," I said pointing to someone else.

"Hmph."

"What?"

"Nothing," he said shaking away a thought. "You're going to want to create a page with a media packet. Include some high resolution shots of the band, some sound clips, maybe some taped interviews if they have any."

"Oh good idea. I don't know why I didn't think of that." I took a notepad off my desk and wrote down his suggestions.

"So, are they our new clients?" he asked.

"No, I'm just helping them out. They're really good. You should come listen. They're playing tonight. You could bring a date."

Trent bit his bottom lip then put a dollar in his jar before storming away.

What did I say?

Chapter 11: Knotted

Bantu Knots: Knots of hair made by wrapping the hair around itself.

~~~

Hair tip #10: To get the most stretch possible, try Bantu knots on dry hair.

~~~

I was trying out a new hairstyle when I went into work that evening. Yeah, I said evening. It was 6pm on a Friday night but I volunteered to set up a profile for a new customer. That meant I had to create a whole new online identity for someone. Sure I could have worked from home, but I decided that actually leaving the house on a Friday night would make me look less pathetic.

Anyway, my hair was in Bantu Knots. I had parted my hair and put in eighteen of those little knots of hair. The cool thing about them was when you undo them in the morning your hair has an awesome wavy texture to it. The uncool thing is that the knots themselves are not very attractive sometimes. But I decided to make it work. I added a pair of big hoop earrings and dressed in my skinny jeans, a pair of cork-heeled sandals, and a fat pattern tunic. The whole effect was this hippie chic look. I kind of stole the style from Marin, but I looked pretty good if I do say so myself.

When I arrived at the office, I was glad that I spent a few extra minutes on my look. Trent Bishop was there. That's not to say that I need to look good for him or anything, but let's face it, you never want to look busted in front of someone of the opposite sex.

"What are you doing here on a Friday night?" I asked as soon as I stepped into the office.

He looked at me strangely. "I'm always here on Friday night. I have no life." I expected him to laugh or something after that remark, but he didn't. He was dead serious. "I like the quiet," he said after a pause. I wasn't sure why he felt the need to explain further.

An hour passed with neither of us speaking to each other. I decided to take a break and snack on the cheese stick I brought. "Want some?" I asked holding it up.

He looked at me suspiciously for a second. Did he think I poisoned it or something? I guess he decided I didn't because he took it out of my hand and started opening it.

So then there we were sitting alone in an office nibbling on cheese sticks as if we were kindergartners or something. Sitting in silence and eating seemed stupid so I decided to start up a conversation.

"So, you have no life," I said. "Me neither."

No response. He just kept eating his cheese. It was awkward to say the least. "So, no girlfriend or anything?

No plans to tie the knot?" I don't know why I kept pushing him. Normally, I would have been perfectly happy sitting in silence. I guessed I was just curious about him. Even though he insisted that it "never happened", I still couldn't forget about how he had concealed my crying in the bathroom. I just wanted to know more about him. But from the way he seemed determined not to utter a single word unless it was absolutely necessary, I was starting to think that wouldn't happen.

"Most people say love is blind," Trent said like ten minutes later. "In my opinion, love is blind, deaf, and dumb." It took me a little while to figure out what the heck he was talking about. It seemed so random, but then I remembered that I had asked him about a girlfriend and tying the knot.

I shook my head. "I swear, you are like a grumpy little old man hiding in a young, sexy body."

"You think I'm sexy?"

"What? Huh?" *Crap. Did I say that out loud?* "Whatever. I didn't say that," I said feigning confidence and indignation. "Stop trying to change the subject. The point is why are you so angry at love? Who chewed up your heart and spit it out?"

Trent didn't respond. He stared at his computer for a long while. I thought the conversation was over until suddenly he said, "April."

"No, it's July," I said thinking he had completely lost his mind. I honestly had almost forgotten what we were talking about. Fortunately, he continued.

"Her name was April. The one who chewed up my heart and spit it out as you so eloquently put it."

"I'm sorry. I didn't know. I was just guessing."

Another silence fell between us. Curiosity was eating me up inside. I really wanted to know what transformed this good-looking and hardworking man into a bitter jerk who was extremely difficult to be around. Finally, I said, "What happened?"

"You ever see those romance movies where the hero runs in and breaks up the wedding of his love and they run off together to live happily ever after?"

I nodded.

"Ever wonder what happens to the poor slub left standing at the altar? He turns into a bitter old man hiding in a sexy body as you so eloquently put it."

"Ouch," I said. I didn't really know how to react to that. I had seen those movies and I often wondered what happened to the other guy. I had always felt bad for him. I never thought I'd be sitting next to 'that guy' at work one day.

I pretended to type at my computer for a while. I needed to write a few pithy and engaging blog posts for my client. But my heart really wasn't in it. All I wanted to do was find out more about Trent and April.

"So another man actually interrupted your wedding?" I asked finally.

He nodded. "And now they're off living happily ever after and I'm stuck paying half the bill for a twenty thousand dollar wedding and honeymoon that never took place. That's where most of the money in that jar goes.

I'm almost finished paying off that honeymoon in the south of France."

Okay, I had to admit, he had a pretty good reason to be angry at love. I think if I was in his situation I would want to curse everyone out all the time as well.

I had no idea what to say. He'd probably heard it all before anyway. Carnece with her wild and slightly violent self would probably spend the next few hours coming up with ways to get revenge on April. She would come up with something creative like hiding a dead fish in her car seats or perhaps using her phone number in an ad for foot fetishes. Marin on the other hand would try to find the bright spot in the entire situation. I tried to go that route.

"Well, at least you're only paying half," I said trying to help. From the way he glared at me, I could tell it didn't work.

"I just broke up with my boyfriend of seven years." I don't know why I told him this. Okay, yes I did. I was trying to make him feel better.

"Why?"

I didn't really want to tell him why. It sounded kind of ridiculous. But since I brought it up, I couldn't really just leave him hanging.

"After seven years, he bought me a house," I said.

"Instead of an engagement ring?"

I looked at him. He got it. He understood. "Yeah." I went back to typing a few almost unintelligible sentences. I couldn't work. I needed a man's opinion on the subject. I really didn't have any other men in my life to talk to. There was my dad and my brother, but that would be like talking to a pair of brick walls. Well-dressed brick walls, but brick walls nonetheless. To them, every single thing in the world could be figured out with a simple pro and con list.

"Do you think I was too harsh on him? I mean, he did buy me a house. Maybe he didn't know I wanted to get married."

"He knew," Trent said not taking his eyes off of his computer screen. "Trust me, a man knows when the woman he's been seeing wants to get married. Women are not the most subtle of our species."

I tried to ignore how he just insulted half the population and thought about what he said. Of course Vinny knew I wanted to get married. Any idiot would be able to figure that out. He just bought that house to placate me. He would never marry me.

My throat tightened and tears threatened.

"Oh no. No. No. No. No crying. I can't deal with crying right now."

I didn't look over at him but I could tell he probably had some stern, cold look on his face.

"I'm not crying," I lied as the first tears seeped out.

Trent switched off his desktop, picked up his laptop case and stood up. "That's it. Let's go."

"What?"

"Get your iPad. You can work on the road."

"On the road? Where are we going?" I asked.

"Out. I'm not going to sit here and watch you cry. It's suffocating. We need air. Let's go."

"Okay." I wiped away my tears, grabbed my iPad and followed him out of the office.

"Go ahead and get your blogs written while I drive. You might want to take a nap, too."

"Nap? How long is this trip? Where the hell are we going?"

"Hey, watch your language before I make you contribute to the jar."

I knew he was joking, but he didn't crack a smile.

I thought I was too curious to fall asleep, but I was wrong. After I typed three of four blog posts, I drifted off. When I woke up, we were at the beach.

"Perfect timing," Trent said, shutting off the engine. He got out the car and then walked around to open my door. "Let's go."

Slightly delirious, I got out of the car and followed him down a slight incline. When I caught up with him, he was lying in a patch of sand staring up at the dark sky. The little area was surrounded by rocks. It was like a private, hidden beach. I sat next to him and hugged my knees. It was kind of chilly.

"This place makes me feel small," he said into the night, well, morning. He scooped up a handful of sand and let it run through his fingers. "Small, like one of these grains of sand. And if *I'm* that small. My problems are even smaller."

I rested my head on my knees and let that sentiment marinate. Normally, someone saying that your problems are no big deal would be kind of offensive. But the way he put it, the whole grains of sand thing, it was kind of beautiful.

"Did you come here with April?" I asked.

Trent shook his head. "She hates sand. And she thinks sea water ruins her hair color."

Ironically, I would have said something similar a few weeks ago. Getting sand or sea water into relaxed hair or weaves is a nightmare. After spending $200 on a weave, you literally protect that thing with your life. It was a huge waste of money and a hassle to clean. But with natural hair it's not that big of a deal. You just wash and go.

I lay down in the sand and watched as the bright spot in the east grew larger and larger. Trent took off his jacket and tossed it to me. "Here, you're shivering."

The next time I looked over at Trent he was sleeping peacefully. I never thought that would be a word I would use to describe Trent. This was a whole other side of him.

~~~

"Mahogany," Trent said when he had woken up. "Mahogany Brown. You realize your name means brown brown."

"Yeah, I know. Vinny calls me Maggie. He thinks Mahogany sounds too formal."

"Well, I don't want to call you the nickname your ex uses."

"My family calls me Michelle sometimes. It's my middle name."

"Ma-hog-any. Any. What about Annie? Does anyone call you that?"

I thought about it for a second. "Nope. I can honestly say that no one has ever thought to call me Annie."

"Well, then that is what I'm going to call you. Annie." He drifted off to sleep again.

~~~

"Thanks," I said on the way home.

"Never happened."

I remembered him using that same phrase when he caught me crying in the bathroom. "Is that how you deal with things now? Anything uncomfortable you just pretend it never happened?"

"Pretty much," he answered.

"That's no way to live life."

"Well, it's worked for the past year and a half."

"So that's it then? For the rest of your life you're just going to hate women, love, and marriage or pretend they don't exist."

"That's the plan," he said.

"Well, that's a crappy plan."

He looked at me as if waiting for me to continue.

"What's that saying?" I asked finally. "Better to have loved and lost than to never have loved at all."

Trent rolled his eyes. Steering the car with his knees for a second, he took out his wallet. After putting a dollar in his pocket he said, "I hate that saying."

"Well, it's true kinda. Just think about what it was like to be in love. The tingly, light headed feeling you get just thinking about them. The way your fingers itch just to touch their skin again. The way you count the minutes until the next time you see their face again."

Instead of answering, Trent just stared at me for a while. Then he said, "But is that worth all the pain that comes if it doesn't work out?"

"Maybe. Maybe not. But you never know until you try."

"There's no maybe about it. It's not worth it. I know from experience, it's not worth it."

Shaking my head, I said, "I don't believe you, Trent Bishop. Anyone who comes up with that 'small grains of sand' line is a romantic at heart.

Suddenly, Trent did something shocking. He smiled and said, "You liked that, huh?"

His tone was almost flirtatious and I actually felt myself blush a little in excitement. I quickly shook it off and said, "Whatever. You know you want a fairytale happily ever after as much as anyone...as much as I do."

Trent's smile quickly faded away as he took in a deep breath and then let it out slowly. He stared at the road and didn't say anything. In fact, he didn't say anything for the rest of the trip. That was one broken man. Of course, he had a reason to be. I wondered if he'd ever be able to get over his heartbreak.

Chapter 12: Puffs

Puffs: A puff ball of hair. Most of the time afro puffs are formed by parting the hair down the middle of the head and tying each section with an elastic.

~~~

Hair tip #11: Try a puff style after the hair has been stretched by a braid out or twist out.

~~~

When you go natural, you go through phases. Sometimes you love your hair, sometimes you hate it. This week I was going through a love phase. I couldn't keep my hands out of my hair. I loved the way it felt soft and squishy in my hands. I loved the texture and everything about it. I loved my two little afro puffs that my hair was styled in. It kind of made me look like a black Princess Leia from Star Wars. I bet Vinny would love it too. He loved Star Wars. This was probably the first hair style since the Big Chop that Vinny would have liked.

Why was I suddenly thinking about him again? It had been almost four months since I had talked to him.

"You are even more adorable than your picture," a female voice said while I was eating my salad in a Georgetown cafe. Apparently, I wasn't the only one who thought I looked cute today.

I looked around for a second. "Are you talking to me?"

She nodded. What did she mean I was more adorable than my picture? Was she trying to hit on me? And why was she taking pictures of me? "I'm sorry, I don't swing that way?"

She looked confused for a second and then shocked. "No, no, that's not what I mean. I'm married. I have no interest in you that way."

"Then what exactly are you talking about?" I asked.

"I'm Seeta. I'm Vinyay's sister."

My mouth flew open. This was his older sister who lived in Canada. I don't know why I didn't recognize her from the pictures I had seen. Maybe because in all the pictures she was dressed in traditional Indian clothing. The girl standing in front of me was modern and stylish. She also didn't look that Indian to me. She could have easily have passed for Hispanic or even Greek.

"Oh, hi, I'm Mahogany." I don't know why I said that. She obviously knew who I was or else she wouldn't have been talking to me in the first place.

I stood up and went to shake her hand but instead she wrapped her arms around me and hugged me. "It is so nice to finally meet you."

"Finally? You mean you knew about me? I had the feeling Vinny hadn't told anyone in his family about me."

She sat down at my table and then waved the waiter over to us. After ordering a drink she said, "Well, he didn't tell me *all* about you. I've known for years that he was in love with a girl he met at school, but it wasn't until he bought a house for you that I saw what you actually looked like."

"Oh, I see. So, he didn't tell you I was black."

She looked down guiltily. "No, he didn't."

"So why are you here? You want to figure out what he saw in me?"

"No, I know what he saw in you. He couldn't stop talking about you. I just wanted to try to explain a little about my brother. I just think you should know some things about him in order to understand him more."

"Like what?" I asked.

"Like that he's a complete coward and an asshole and honestly I'm not sure what *you* ever saw in him."

Okay, I have to admit, I didn't see that coming at all.

Seeta's drink order arrived and she took a long swig before continuing. "If he really wanted to marry you, he could have done it a long time ago. He is just blaming it on your race and tradition because he is completely afraid of commitment."

"I'm so confused. I thought you two were close. Why are you bad mouthing him to me?"

"Don't get me wrong. I totally love my brother, but come on. He's like a ten year old. He can't even commit to a favorite flavor of gum let alone to a woman."

"So it's not actually against your religion or culture or anything to marry outside of your race?"

"Well, yeah, it kind of is, but rules are made to be broken and people break them all the time. We have a cousin who married an Italian. It's shocking at first but people get over it. They would get over it with you and Vinny as well."

I wasn't quite sure how Seeta was helping Vinny's case. I mean what was she really saying? Sure my family is going to hate you, but they'll deal with it as long as my brother really wants you which he obviously doesn't since he didn't marry you.

"What about you? How do you feel about me being with your brother?"

She took a deep breath. One of those breaths that was usually followed by bad news.

"I have to be honest with you," she said after a moment. "When I first found out you weren't Indian, I told Vinny to dump you immediately."

"Great." I rolled my eyes and started to stand. I didn't have to hear this. I was just starting to get my confidence back and here she was trying to tell me that I wasn't good enough for someone in her family. Seeta grabbed my hand and begged me with her eyes to sit back down again.

"But," she said squeezing my hand. "He didn't. Instead, he bought you a house. That tells me a lot about how he feels about you."

"I never asked him to buy me a house." Why did everyone keep using that as the measuring stick for his love for me? It seemed like that was the important thing to everyone, but not to me. To me the important thing was that he hid my race from his family for seven freaking years!

"I really don't understand what you're trying to tell me here."

Seeta sighed. "I'm saying that Vinyay really loves you. He just hasn't realized how much. Give him some time to grow. I'm sure you two can work it out."

I wasn't so sure about that. But it did give me a little tingly feeling inside to know that I had finally met someone in Vinny's family and that she actually supported our relationship. It made me feel like Vinny and I had a chance after all.

Chapter 13: Finger Coils

Finger Coils: Style formed by dividing the hair into small sections and then coiling the hair around the finger.

~~~

Hair tip #12: Coils work best on freshly washed and conditioned hair. You may also want to use a mousse or gel to help them stay in place and give them a shiny finish.

~~~

I have to give it to Marin. When she decides to do something, she's all in. Cutting her hair may have looked like a spur of the moment thing, but since then she had made it the focus of her life. She had joined me in watching the YouTube videos, but she had also started reading books and magazines and even attending a natural hair support group. Yes, there was a group for black women to help each other get through the tough times of natural hair care. And yes there were some difficult times.

"You can't give up," Marin said one night when I had decided to get a relaxer. "I'm coming over."

Two hours later she was in my apartment lecturing me about hair care.

"It's just too hard," I said near tears. "I can't do it anymore. I'm just going to get a relaxer and it will be so much easier."

"Easier? It won't be easier. It will just be the same. It's just what you're used to."

Marin sat her cooler filled with milk and ginger beer on my coffee table. "Do you know why natural hair *seems* so hard? It's because we've never learned how to deal with our own hair. We've had weaves and perms and Jheri curls all our lives. We know how to deal with processed hair, although not very well. Maybe if we started dealing with our *own* hair from the time we were little, we would be better prepared to deal with it when we are adults."

"So what am I supposed to do? Spend three hours a day grooming my hair because that's the way it's supposedly supposed to be. What about what's easy? What about what I have *time* to do?"

"This is bigger than you, don't you see?" she asked. I wasn't sure if it was a rhetorical question or not.

"No, sorry. What am I supposed to see?"

"That we have to take the power. As a people we have to stop believing that we are not good enough, that our hair is not good enough. Do you realize that black women are the only women on the planet who systematically try to chemically or physically change the structure of their hair?

"That's not true."

"Think about it. It is. As a race, we have passed on from generation to generation the fundamental idea that our hair, the way it grows out of our head, is not good enough. We have to do something to it."

I tried to dispute her, but I couldn't. Sure women of other cultures occasionally got curly perms or flat ironed their hair or colored it. But we were the only ones who did it systematically. It was ingrained in us from infancy that our nappy hair had to be changed.

"Also, think about this," Marin continued. "African women are the only women on the planet with this texture of hair. Maybe we should start celebrating our hair as unique and special instead of treating it as a nuisance. Tell me, has anyone asked to touch your hair since your big chop?"

Actually several curious people, mostly white, but some black, have asked if they could touch it to see what it felt like. Sometimes it got downright annoying.

I nodded to Marin.

"Now, had anyone ever asked to touch your hair when it was relaxed or when you had a weave."

I shook my head.

"So what does that tell you?" she asked by way of summary.

"That people are weird and nosey."

"Or that your hair is special and so are you." She gave me a knowing look as if her words had deeper meaning.

"Okay, you don't have to turn all psychiatrist on me," I said looking away.

"Well, I think maybe I do. This is what we go through all the time in my hair therapy group. For some women, their entire self-worth and self-esteem is tied up with their hair. I think you might be one of those women."

"Are you saying I'm never going to be able to like myself until I like my hair?" I asked.

Marin shrugged. "Maybe partially."

"That's ridiculous Marin."

"Is it? Is it ridiculous to think that when a woman looks in the mirror and doesn't like what she sees that it might have something to do with the way she feels about herself, the decisions she makes, or the men she chooses."

I was getting slightly tired of the lecturing, but she did it in such a caring and concerned way, it was hard to be angry with her. It was even harder to tell her to stop. Especially since I was starting to think she had a point.

"It's not about equating your hair to your self-worth. It's about being able to look in the mirror and like what you see. When you can't do that, it causes so many other problems in all aspects of your life. Your hair is more than your hair. It is your self-image and identity."

"But I used to be able to do that when I had my weave. I liked what I saw all the time."

"Then why did you cut it off?"

"I cut it off because I was pissed at Vinny."

"I don't believe that," she said shaking her head. "I think you cut it off because deep down you finally wanted to be yourself. Once you accept that your hair is never going to be like white hair you're going to be happy. Just like when you finally accept that you are never going to be what Vinny wants you to be."

This was hard to hear. I tried not to believe it but I had to. I was never going to be Indian like Vinny wanted me to be in order to marry me and my hair was never going to be straight, not naturally that is. In order to make it straight, I'd have to do constant irreversible damage to my hair.

I sat silent in my living room as I stared in the mirror at my short nappy hair. It was going to take some serious mental retraining in order to start thinking of my hair as special and unique instead of ethnic and ugly. I tried to concentrate on all the compliments I had received lately. I never received compliments on my hair before. Now my hair was something different that people weren't used to. Different wasn't always bad.

"Fine, I'll stick it out," I said, finally relenting to her way of thinking.

Marin let out a sigh of relief. "Good. Good. And I think maybe you should come to my support group with me."

"All the way in Philly? I don't have time for that."

"Come on, it will give you a chance to come see your brother. And you can help me set up the baby room."

I shrugged not willing to give her a firm commitment. Driving two states away just to hear a group of women whine about their hair was not near the top of my to-do list.

"Now let's see what we can do with your hair," Marin said. "I have a great idea for a style. We can brush it out section by section and then put finger curls in it with gel. Your hair is the perfect length for it and it will look great.

I sat back and closed my eyes as Marin got started on my transformation.

~~~

Two weeks later there was a hair show in Atlanta. Marin and I decided to make a girls' weekend out of it. We tried to invite Carnece but she had a completely different concept about hair.

"Hair is an accessory," she said. "An accessory like my shoes. If I don't like my shoes you don't see me getting all weepy over it. I just go out and buy another pair. It's the same with my hair. If I don't like it one day, I buy a new wig."

"Yes, but don't you want your own hair?" Marin had asked her.

"It *is* my hair. I have the receipt," Carnece said with a 'duh' look on her face.

It was at this hair expo that I think my eyes were finally opened about this whole hair revolution thing. There was a change brewing. I saw so many different hair textures and styles and so much pride. People were proud of their hair whether it was short, long, curly, or kinky. I saw products that were created *by* black people *for* black people. Products that the creators had used on their own hair and thus could give advice on specific hair care techniques. No products from major corporations who didn't even have a black employee. That was something that had always secretly bothered me about the hair care industry. I mean, black women only made up about 8% of the buying population, but they bought 90% of the products. Change was coming and change looked good.

Chapter 14: Shrinkage

Shrinkage: Because of the tight curl pattern of African American hair, much length is lost due to what is called shrinkage. Especially after washing, hair can lose several inches in visible length due to shrinkage. One of the first steps to natural hair care is finding a healthy way to stretch the hair and give it length.

~~~

Hair tip #13: Styling dry hair keeps it from shrinking as much. Hair should be dry but well-oiled and moisturized before attempting things like twist outs and braid outs.

~~~

My hair was finally growing. I could tell. When I sat in front of the mirror and stretched out one of the tightly curled strands of hair, I could see how long it was. Unfortunately, as soon as I released the hair it shriveled up against my head again making it look like I had no hair at all.

Shrinkage

I had no idea how I was going to style my hair for my date with James. I didn't know why I was so worried about it. On our two previous dates, he didn't seem to mind my natural hair. In fact, he loved it. He often introduced me as his naturally beautiful black queen. I guess that was one benefit to dating a black man. I knew that if I was with Vinny, I would constantly have to explain this transformation my hair was undergoing. He completely wouldn't understand why it suddenly wasn't straight anymore.

"Honestly, I'm so happy we're together now," James with two 'A's said.

Together? We had been on three dates spread out over a month and hadn't done more than a little front door kissing that I actually didn't find too exciting. Did that mean we were a couple? I really didn't know. Maybe that was how things worked nowadays. After a few dates there was an understood agreement that you were a couple. That didn't sound quite right to me. That really didn't seem like the way things went with Carnece.

"Um, why?" I asked not knowing what else to say.

"I've seen you around the neighborhood before with an Indian looking man. Was he your man before?"

I nodded.

James with two 'A's shook his head. "You see that is what is wrong with our people."

"Our people?"

"Yes, black people. Always trying to date outside of our race. It's disrespectful."

I almost choked on my chicken. "Disrespectful? To who?"

"To us. How are we supposed to teach a new generation of young people to have pride in their skin color if our own people don't? When you date someone of another race, it's like saying that your own people aren't good enough."

I was too shocked to speak. I knew some people felt that way, but I had never actually met someone. I thought it was only some white people who were against interracial dating. I didn't know there were some black people who felt that way as well. I guess you could call this reverse racism. Wait a minute. That term didn't sit right with me. It was like saying that white people being racist toward black was the right way, but black racism toward white was backwards. All racism is wrong no matter what direction it goes.

I put my fork down and as calmly as possible said, "So let's say hypothetically that we have a child and he or she falls in love with someone of a different skin color. You would forbid them from marrying?"

"Absolutely," Jaames said without hesitation. "All of my children know that's unacceptable. A quick fling is one thing, but marriage or procreation is completely out of the question."

My heartbeat accelerated. Some women might not have been as offended as I was in that moment. They could have thought of it as a compliment that a black man thought black women were the only women worthy enough for him. Especially considering the way the rest of society considered black women. But for me, I couldn't help wondering if Vinny's family might have had conversations exactly like this. If Vinny was raised in a similar environment, then it perfectly explained why marriage to me never even crossed his mind.

Wait a minute. What was that he had said about children? "Your children know it's unacceptable? You have children?"

"Yeah, I do," he said simply as if it was common knowledge. "I have eleven."

"Eleven? You have eleven children?"

He nodded. "And I hope to have many more. Children are a beautiful thing don't you agree?"

"Yeah and blue birds are beautiful too but that doesn't mean I want eleven of them!"

James with two 'A's laughed. "You are too cute. We are going to be good together."

And what exactly did that mean? Was he planning on knocking me up a few times? Was that his idea of good?

Needless to say, I was a bit distracted for the rest of the date. James with two 'A's was a little too much for me to handle. He was beyond too much to handle, he was insane. Why would he think I'd want to get involved with someone who had eleven kids? I had to find a way out of this relationship that was apparently started without my knowledge.

"Once I see a woman that I know will make beautiful babes, I don't leave her alone until we have those babies. I'm like a lion on the prowl." He smiled at me as if that was some sort of sexy pick up line. Did women actually go for that? Apparently so. It had worked at least eleven other times.

"Don't worry, it's not like I'm a dead beat dad or anything. I support all of my kids. And I'll support you as well. That's why I work so hard. Gotta support my families."

This was actually the first time we had a date that didn't revolve around one of his performances. Maybe that was why the eleven kid thing hadn't come up before. He had just called me this morning and asked if we could have lunch. And now in the middle of lunch, I had really lost my appetite.

Just out of curiosity I decided to probe a little further in to James' ideas. "So how do you feel about Halle Berry?"

"She looks too Caucasian for my tastes but I can see how some men find her attractive."

Some men? Well, that was an understatement.

"So you're saying you would kick Halle Berry out of your bed if she decided to climb in there one day for some reason."

"Now, I'm not saying all that. I'm just saying I wouldn't want to procreate with her for fear that our children would come out too Caucasian."

"Right. Procreate. Right," I said nodding. He had a right to be wrong. No problem. Just not with me. But the whole Halle Berry conversation gave me an excellent idea.

When it was time to head back to the office, I asked James with two 'A's to walk me back. And then I invited him up. I knew Trent would be at his desk. He rarely took lunch out of the office. I didn't know whether it was because he was cheap or because he always had a website to maintain.

Once we were inside, I wrapped my arms around Trent's neck and gave him a kiss on the cheek.

"What are you doing?" he asked nearly jumping out of his seat.

I laughed. "Oh he hates when I do that at work. Jaames, I'd like to introduce you to my brother Trent."

"Brother?" Jaames said looking totally confused. "But he's white. You mean step brother or adopted brother?"

"No. Biological brother. Our mother is white and our father is black. Genes are a funny thing aren't they?"

"So you're half white?"

I nodded. Trent just stared at me with his classic half blank and half angry glare. I ignored him. He'd get over it.

"I never would have guessed you were half white with your hair texture," Jaames continued.

"Well, I am. I completely understand if you don't want to see me anymore. I mean we all have our standards. I mean what if we had a child together like you've planned. God forbid your thirteenth child come out with blue eyes like my brother Trent here." I pet Trent on the head like he was a cocker spaniel or something.

Trent's eyes expanded as he stared back and forth between Jaames and me for a moment. I had no idea what was going on in his head, but I was sure he would let me know later on.

"Twelfth. It would just be my twelfth child," Jaames said as if he was contemplating the possibility.

"Oh, yeah, right, my bad."

"Well, I better get going," Jaames said inching his way to the door. "Are you coming to my show tonight?"

"I don't know. Trent, aren't we supposed to go out with mom tonight?"

Trent squinted and scrunched up his nose as if he had just swallowed rancid sushi. I thought sure my whole plan was blown. There was no way he was gonna help me out. But then he took a deep breath, shook his head and said, "Yeah, that's right. We're having dinner together at seven...with mom. Our mom." Trent rolled his eyes as if he couldn't believe he was playing along.

"Sorry, Jaames. Maybe another time. Call me okay?"

Jaames gave a dismissive wave and left.

After he was gone I let out a huge sigh of relief. Trent was staring at me again.

"Okay, let me explain," I said preemptively.

Trent held up his hand. "I don't even want to know."

Chapter 15: *Afro*

Afro: Do I really need to define afro? I don't think so.

~~~

Hair tip #14: I have found that a good old fashioned springy afro pick works best at getting the full-on Angela Davis fro look.

~~~

*N*o one is going to understand your costume," Marin said as she waddled down the street next to me. She was seven months pregnant but wasn't going to let that stop her from a night of partying. I didn't mind. I needed to go to this office party and I really didn't want to do it alone. Besides, I kind of liked partying with Marin. She was like a PG version of Carnece. Just as extreme and daring but she didn't need any alcohol to make her act like a lunatic. She was just naturally crazy and it was pretty fun to watch.

"Everyone is going to get it. Well, at least the black people," I said in response.

"You look like a glow worm with a sponge hat."

"And you look like a bag lady. A pregnant bag lady." Marin laughed and slipped her arm through mine.

"Come on, let's go get our party on."

Yes, we were in costumes, but it wasn't Halloween. Mr. George, our quirky boss only allowed three office parties a year. For each party he would randomly choose a holiday, theme, and a date. So tonight we were celebrating Arbor Day with a costume party in September. It was so bizarre that I refused to go alone. Marin happily volunteered.

How exactly do you celebrate Arbor Day with a party? Apparently by decorating the office with trees made of green construction paper and serving green drinks while people stood around in costumes completely unrelated to trees. Honestly, I swear this whole thing was an excuse for my boss to wear a loin cloth and call himself George of the Jungle.

"Wow, who is that?' Marin asked as she sipped her thermos of milk that she'd brought from home. She never trusted that the place she was going would have milk for her. Even if they had milk, she didn't trust it to be organic. I had seen this woman eat Roti off the floor of a food truck, but God forbid the milk not come from grass fed cows.

"Who?" I asked trying to follow her line of sight. My gaze landed on a man wearing a hat and tight pants. His back was turned to me so I couldn't tell who it was. But I honestly couldn't remember any one in the office having a butt that amazing.

"Look at that ass," Marin continued. "It's so tight if you pinch it you might break a nail."

I stared at her in shock. "Marin! You're married. To my brother. And you're pregnant!"

"You have no idea what these pregnancy hormones do to me. I'm horny *all* the time."

"Stop. Please, stop. That is so gross," I said holding up my hand.

"Well, let's go meet him."

Before I could stop her, she had started walking straight toward him. To make matters worse, the man in tight pants turned slightly and I thought I recognized him. For a second, I actually thought I was looking at Trent.

"Marin, wait. What are you -" It was too late. Marin had walked up to the man and introduced herself. When he turned around to shake her hand, I nearly tripped over the snack table. It was Trent.

"I don't actually work here. My sister-in-law does," she was saying by the time I reached them.

Trent smiled at me. I had worked with him for almost two years and I wasn't even sure if he had teeth. A year ago when Mr. George decided that the entire office should go from desks to bean bags we were the only ones who refused. Since then, we'd had desks right next to each other but that didn't mean we actually talked or anything. In fact, I didn't know anything about him besides his money jar and his failed engagement. Now, I could add the fact that he had a fantastic ass.

"Sweet Mahogany, how ya doin?" he asked wrapping one arm around me in sort of a side hug. Okay, this was weird. "Your sister-in-law is the only person in this place with any sense," Trent said to Marin. He let me go and then held out his hand to her again. Did he forget he already shook her hand? "I'm Trent."

"Nice to meet you," she said as Trent took a sip of his drink. That's when I figured it out. He was drunk. Which confused me. Most people got obnoxious and annoying when they drink. Alcohol seemed to have the opposite effect on Trent. He was downright...pleasant. It was kind of unsettling.

"Let me guess," Marin said, looking at his costume up and down. Taking in his black shirt unbuttoned to his navel she asked, "Are you a stripper?"

Trent beamed. He was rather attractive when he smiled. A sexy five-o'clock shadow framed his full pink lips. I subconsciously licked my own lips wondering how my tongue would feel against his. I hoped he didn't notice.

"Nope," he said holding in a drunken giggle. He pointed to a brown handprint on his chest and to the badge on his shirt. "I'm a dirty cop." Trent fell into uncontrollable giggles. I smiled not able to hold in a giggle myself. It kind of made me happy that he was happy.

"Nice. Nice," Marin said. I had the feeling Marin was commenting more on his physique than on the cleverness of his costume.

"What about you?" he asked her when he had gotten control of himself. "What's with the stuffed animal paws? Are you some sort of animal serial killer?"

Afro

"No. I'm pregnant and these are paws." she said pointing to a particularly odd looking teddy bear paw. "Get it? I'm a pregnant pause."

Trent started laughing again. "That's priceless. Love it. Great costume. Although I'm not quite sure what costumes or cheap rum have to do with Arbor Day."

"That's exactly what Mahogany said. Isn't that right?" she asked looking at me.

Unfortunately, I was incapable of speaking. And it wasn't only because I had just discovered that Trent had an amazing body. I think the fact that he was able to have a polite conversation with someone was even more shocking. He wasn't being insulting or vulgar.

"And what are you?" Trent asked smiling at me again. His eyes were sparkling and warm. I started to see him in a new light.

"Um," I said.

"I told her no one would get it. She's wearing shiny clothing and she has an afro."

"Afro-sheen," he said immediately.

"You know what that is?" Marin asked.

He nodded. "Yep." After finishing off his drink, he added. "I'm thirsty. Can I get you anything?"

"Um," I said.

"I'm good." Marin held up her thermos. "Get Mahogany a screwdriver."

"Got it," he said before heading to the bar.

"What in the world was that?" I asked Marin once Trent had left.

Marin didn't answer. She was too busy watching Trent walk away.

"Marin!" I yelled as I smacked her on the arm. "You're a married woman! Married to my brother."

Marin whipped out her phone. After swiping it on and pressing a button, she said, "Honey, time to break out the honey."

"Gross," I said.

"I'm out. I gotta go. I need it now."

"I really didn't need to know that. Honey? Seriously?"

Chugging her milk, Marin made her way through the crowd and toward the exit.

"Crap. She drove," I said as I watched her leave.

"What?" Trent asked, handing me my drink.

"Oh, nothing." Not realizing how thirsty I was, I drank the entire screwdriver in three gulps.

"Wanna dance?"

"What?"

Before I could protest, Trent swept me up into his arms and led me to the dance floor. Or shall I say the center of the bean bag circle.

I used to love to dance, but Vinny was never any good at it so I didn't get to do it very often. If we were out together, Vinny never wanted to dance with me and he got extremely jealous if I danced with anyone else. So the only time I got to get my groove on was when I was out with my girls and that wasn't very often.

That night, I think I lost count of how many times I was surprised by Trent. He was an awesome dancer. He had this laid back kind of swag about him. He was able to show off his rhythm without seeming like he was trying too hard.

Afro

He grabbed my hand, spun me around and then kept swaying to the music. Don't ask me what song was playing. I wouldn't be able to tell you. It was kind of fast, kind of slow, and a lot in between.

At first I felt awkward because there wasn't anyone else dancing...well there could have been and I just didn't notice. Anyway, no one could be dancing because I was positive everyone was staring at us. After the first song ended and Trent melded into the next without missing a step, I noticed something. People weren't staring at me, they were staring at Trent.

By the end of the next song, I was being pushed out of the way by other girls who wanted their turn with him.

Two hours later, Trent was still dancing. He had only left the floor twice and that was just to go to the bathroom. He didn't need to leave the floor to get a drink refill. Everywhere he turned there was another girl waiting to hand him one.

I stood by the bar unable to take my eyes off of him. Not because I was attracted to him or anything. In fact, I was merely starting to get a little worried for him. After what I counted to be his sixth drink since getting on the dance floor, I heard someone yell, "Take it off, Trent!" Followed by several voices chanting his name.

Trent might not have been my favorite person in the office. Okay, honestly, most of the time I hated his guts, but I wouldn't wish this on anyone. How would he be able to show his face at work again if he ended up stripping in front of everyone? And we were a social media firm. Pictures of his ass would be on Facebook before his pants hit the ground.

I had to put an end to this. And there was only one thing I could think of that would tear horny twenty-year-old white girls away from the prospect of a hot guy going all "Magic Mike" on them.

"Oh my God! Is that Taylor Swift?" I yelled while looking out of the window. "It is! It is Taylor Swift!"

When the girls started stampeding to the window like a bunch of drunken cattle, I grabbed Trent by the arm and led him toward the door.

"Whoa, hey, can you slow down?" Trent said once we made it outside. "Oh and tell the Earth to stop spinning so fast or something." Trent giggled uncontrollably. It was such a happy little giggle that I almost giggled as well. But this was no time for laughter. I needed to get this man home before he passed out. I knew I would not be strong enough to carry him.

"How did you get here?" I asked.

"Drove."

"How were you planning to get home?"

Trent started steering an imaginary wheel like he was in a video game. He stepped off the curb and straight into oncoming traffic.

I pulled him out of the way and said, "Well, you're not driving anywhere. Give me your keys."

"Yes, ma'am," he said with a mock salute. "I would give you anything."

"Whatever, Drunk Boy." I snatched the keys out of his hand and said, "Let's go."

I didn't know where he parked so I clicked the panic button on his key chain and followed the sound of the blaring alarm while Trent leaned on me with nearly all of his weight on my shoulder.

"All right, now where do you live?" I asked once we were finally in the car. Instead of answering, Trent just started singing "Panama" by Van Halen.

Great. He was in no condition to tell me where he lived. Where was I supposed to take him?

I stared at the steering wheel as Trent serenaded me with the Kit Kat bar jingle. I guess I had no choice but to take him to my place.

Chapter 16: Bed Head

Bed head: Sleeping on natural hair without prepping it leads to what I call bed head. Your hair is coarse and matted to your head. Basically, it is not in any state for public viewing.

~~~

Hair tip #15: If you happened to fall asleep without braiding, twisting, or banding your hair first, try wetting it in the shower and blowing it out on a low setting.

~~~

*T*rent didn't stop singing all the way to my apartment. I don't think he knew where he was or where he was going, but he really didn't care. He was just plain happy.

Once we were upstairs in my apartment I said, "Alright, you can have the couch."

"Awesome," he said giving me the thumbs up.

"Well, I'm going to sleep."

"Sleep later. Let's dance." He wrapped his arms around me and started swaying to nonexistent music.

"Trent, there's no music." I started to push him back toward the couch.

"I can sing."

"Yes, I know that. You've been singing for the last twenty minutes. I think it's time to sleep now."

He let me go and said, "Yeah, you're probably right. Where am I?"

"You're at my place. You're too drunk to drive and I didn't know where you lived."

Taking off his shirt he said, "Okay." He shrugged and plopped on the couch.

He was so easy going like this. I didn't know how I would be able to go back to the old Trent.

I started to walk away when he grabbed my hand and pulled me back. "Thank you, Mahogany," he said suddenly sounding sober.

"You're welcome." I tried to pull my hand away but he had a tight grip. For the first time that night, I realized what I had just done. I had brought a drunk man that I barely knew into my home. What was I thinking? What if he tried to hurt me? I hadn't even considered that possibility. Now I started to get a little frightened. But what he did next shocked me even more.

He kissed my hand and said, "I love you."

I laughed. I knew he was talking crazy. I knew for a fact that he had no interest in black girls. Wow, alcohol turned him into a completely different person. "You're drunk, Trent. Just go to sleep."

Pulling me down on top of him, he stared into my eyes and said, "I might be drunk, but I know what I'm saying. I love you. I love everything about you. I love your smile. I love your laugh. I love your hair." He smiled at me like a child and said, "Can I touch it? I've always wanted to touch it."

Too shocked to speak I just nodded.

How did I get into this position? Lying on top of a drunk man who was now playing in my hair. My chest was on top of his moving in rhythm. His right hand was on the small of my back keeping me in place as his left hand squeezed the curls of my afro. I should have gotten off of him, but I had to admit, it felt kind of good. My hand secretly rubbed against the muscles of his chest.

"It's so soft," he whispered. Trent leaned forward and took in a deep breath. "It smells good too."

"Thanks?" It was more of a question than a statement. I was just so completely confused.

Leaning back again, he said, "You have this black freckle on the right side of your neck that might be the sexiest thing I have ever seen in my life." He gently rubbed the right side of my neck and added, "I daydream about it so much that sometimes I can't get any work done."

It was a cute little confession of love, but I knew he was just drunk. He wouldn't remember any of this in the morning. But since I hadn't had a warm body under me in a while, I just played along.

"Really, Trent? And how long have you had these feelings for me?"

Trent closed his eyes and started breathing evenly. I thought he had fallen asleep until he opened his eyes and said, "Six months, two weeks, and five days."

Bed Head

That's when I realized he was serious. I hopped up off of him and said, "Good night, Trent." But as I went to sleep that night, I tried my best to think about what happened six months, two weeks, and five days ago that would cause him to feel this way.

~~~

When you go natural, you can't really just go to bed and wake up expecting to be able to manage your hair in the morning. You see, what happens is, your hair gets all flat and matted as you sleep. Last night my hair was a nice fluffy afro. This morning it looked like two inches of black knots. I yawned and stretched then grabbed my moisturizer. Good thing it was a Saturday. It was going to take me a good three hours to get my hair soft again.

Soft. Someone else had just called my hair soft. Trent. He spent the night, didn't he? I peeked my head through my bedroom door and got a glimpse of the tall half naked man sleeping on my couch.

What on Earth was I thinking? How could I let a drunk stranger just spend the night? Was I drunk too?

Trent moaned and I slammed my door shut. I couldn't let him see me like this. I had to figure out something to do with my hair. Even though I really didn't care what Trent thought of me, no one deserved to see me with bed head. It was a pretty tragic sight.

Although considering what he told me last night, maybe he needed to see me like this. That would cure whatever infatuation he thought he had with me.

I shook my head. What he said last night was just the ramblings of an intoxicated fool. There was no way Trent Bishop had any real feelings for me.

I spritzed my hair with my water and coconut oil mixture. Once it was saturated, I worked my crème moisturizer through it. Slowly I molded my hair into something more appealing.

My hair was still too tightly coiled to make a nice afro puff. So instead, I made a part down the middle of my head and created two little afro puffs.

When I finished, I opened my door a crack and peeked through. Trent hadn't moved. Maybe I should check for a pulse, I thought. Of course, I decided against it. I didn't want to get too close to his naked chest again.

Instead, I went to the kitchen and started a pot of coffee. When it was finished, I brought a cup over to the couch. I stared at him for a while. Breathing in and out. There was still a streak of dirt on his chest from his dirty cop costume. Most of it had been wiped away while he was dancing with every girl in the office. Or I guess it could have come off while I was lying on top of him last night.

Okay, I needed to stop thinking about him like this. That meant he needed to get up. Now.

I reached over and nudged his shoulder. He groaned and turned over. I thumped him in the head. Nothing. I needed to get serious. I held his coffee cup next to his head and then flicked some of the liquid on him with my finger. That did it.

"Stop. What are you doing?" he whined in a husky voice as he put his arm over his face.

"It's time to wake up, Trent."

I saw his back tense up at the sound of my voice. He rolled on to his back and stared straight up at the ceiling as if he was afraid to look around.

"Where am I?" he asked blinking rapidly. Apparently, my ceiling looked somehow different from his own.

"You're at my place."

"Mahogany," he said without looking at me. It wasn't a question. It was like he knew exactly who I was just by the sound of my voice. He didn't even sound surprised. "Oh God, what did I do?" He sat up quickly then grabbed his head and lay back down.

Instead of answering, I sipped my coffee. I thought he'd need a few sips of coffee before he heard about how he almost stripped in front of the entire office.

A few moments later, Trent turned and looked at me through his fingers. "Did we...did we ... you know?"

"No, we didn't."

He sighed. "Thank God."

"Hey, what's that supposed to mean?" I asked slightly offended.

"No....I didn't mean..." He closed his eyes and sat up slowly this time. Once he was in a seated position he took a sip of coffee then he said, "Trust me, if we had done something, you'd be regretting it much more than I would."

Now I was even more confused. "What's that supposed to mean? Do you have an STD or something?"

Trent choked on his coffee. "No...No...I just...Look let's start over. Uh, why am I here?"

"You were too drunk to drive and I didn't know where you lived."

"Oh." He took another sip of coffee. "Thank you."

We sat in awkward silence for a while.

"I bet I was out of control last night," he said finally.

"You were...interesting," I said unable to think of a more appropriate word. I could have said he was nice, amiable, conversational, or pleasant. But that didn't seem like a good way to describe someone who was blackout drunk.

"Interesting?" he asked calling my bluff.

"Well, talkative," I added.

He paled. Which was pretty hard to do considering he was already pretty pale. He just turned downright ghostly.

"Did I...say anything... um... to you?"

I thought about rubbing his proclamation of love to me in his face, but that would have been cruel. I could tell by the fearful look in his eyes that he obviously didn't mean it. He would have been horrified and embarrassed.

I also had to remember that we worked together. If it ever got out what he said last night, even if it was false, it might still be awkward between us. If I kept it to myself, we might be able to go back to our strained, slightly polite work relationship. With all this in mind, I answered his question.

"No, you didn't say anything in particular to me."

He let out a big sigh of relief. "Good, that's good," he said, setting down his cup of coffee and looking around my couch.

"Your shirt is there," I said pointing to where it was sticking out from under the cushion.

"Thanks. I'm just going to wash up and, uh, get out of your hair," he said standing. "Bathroom?"

"First door on the left."

As soon as he went into the bathroom, there was a knock on my door.

"Vinny?" I said when I answered it.

"Hey, Mags," he said.

I looked at my watch. I couldn't remember the last time Vinny was out of bed before eleven let alone at 7:58 in the morning. This had to be important.

"Are you okay?" I asked a little worried.

"Yeah, I'm fine. Totally, fine. I'm seeing someone."

"Good. Good for you." Of course, I didn't mean that. He was my ex. Of course, I wanted him to be miserable for the rest of his life. But the way he said it kind of made me think he was lying. Why would he volunteer that information literally three seconds after I opened the door?

"You seeing anyone?" he asked suspiciously. Did he really just knock on my door at eight am on a Saturday to inquire about my love life?

"No," I said simply. I should have lied, too, but I didn't see the need. I was above stupid little games. "So, why are you here so early in the morning? What do you want?" I asked. His presence was actually starting to annoy me.

"It took a while, but I finally got the house in order. You know, our house," he said.

I rolled my eyes. "I never asked you for a house. It's not *our* house. It's *your* house."

"Maggie, don't be like this. You know I bought it for *us*. You know how I feel about you. It's been six months and I still feel the same."

This was so not a good time. I was just at the point when I thought I could actually get over him and move on. For a second I thought I might even be into Trent. Oh God. Trent was still here.

As soon as I thought his name he emerged from the bathroom as if I had summoned him from my mind.

"Who is that?" Vinny said pushing past me.

This was so not happening.

"You must be Vinny," Trent said calmly as he buttoned his shirt.

This looked bad. This looked so bad. I'm sure Vinny assumed Trent had spent the night...which he had, but it was completely innocent.

"I'm Trent," he said after he finished the last button. He held out his hand and added, "I work with Mahogany."

Vinny slapped his hand away. "What are you doing in my...What are you doing in her apartment?"

Trent looked at me. "Is he serious?"

I started to get a little nervous. Vinny was being a total jerk and I wasn't sure what version of Trent I was facing. Was it the friendly drunk from last night, or was he going to be the usual foul-mouthed obnoxious asshole I was used to. In either case, I needed to put an end to this before someone got hurt. And given the size of Trent, I had a sneaky suspicion it would be Vinny.

Bed Head

"We had an office party last night. Trent was too drunk to drive so he stayed over. Nothing happened," I said trying to calm the waters a bit.

"Mahogany, you don't owe him any explanation," Trent said with a smirk. "You two aren't together anymore."

What exactly was he trying to do? He needed to stay out of this before things got bad.

"You need to mind your business, pretty boy," Vinny said.

"Aw, he thinks I'm pretty. Now, I know why you're not together. I think he's on the wrong team, Mahogany." Trent laughed as he tucked in his shirt.

Vinny didn't think it was the slightest bit funny as evidenced by the punch he threw at Trent's face.

Oh Lord, drama. There was about to be a knock down drag out fight right there in my living room.

But to my surprise, Trent didn't retaliate. He rubbed his jaw for a second and then said, "See you Monday, Mahogany," before grabbing his keys and leaving.

Chapter 17: Hair Accessories

Hair Accessories: This doesn't mean your run of the mill scrunchies or head bands. With curly textured hair, you can really get creative with hair accessories and turn a potential bad hair day into a hair victory. Get creative. Anything from flowers to scarves to even jewelry can be a hair accessory.

~~~

I dreaded seeing Trent that Monday morning. I didn't know why really. It wasn't like we had done anything. Now *that* would be awkward. I still didn't understand how coworkers were able to casually sleep together one night and then look at each other the next day at work. The thought kind of grossed me out.

Anyway, I didn't want to see Trent because I was just really embarrassed at how Vinny had behaved. I still couldn't believe he had punched Trent. Seeta was right. Vinny was like a ten-year-old. And I was like one of his toys. An accessory. He didn't want me, but he also didn't want anyone else to have me.

But as hard as it was to believe that Vinny had punched Trent, it was even harder to believe that Trent hadn't punched him back. I mean, I had gotten a glimpse of Trent's physique that night and he definitely had all the equipment to put Vinny in a world of hurt, but he didn't.

I tried to sleep in Monday morning. For me that means 7 a.m. I usually hop out of bed at six no matter what. That morning I forced myself to stay in bed until seven. I dressed slowly and took my time with breakfast. Even moving at a snail's pace, I was still ready to leave the house at eight which meant I would get to work by 8:30. Still too early. I didn't want to run the risk of having too much alone time with Trent. And considering that most of our coworkers had now started arriving at 9:30 or 10, I decided to try to delay myself even more.

Apparently, Trent and I thought too much alike because even though we both usually get to work about a quarter to 8, that Monday morning we both arrived at 9:15.

Trent and I hesitated at the elevator door. What if it broke down again and we were stuck alone for an hour.

"I'm going to take the stairs," he said when the elevator arrived on the ground floor.

"Don't be ridiculous, Trent. Just get in."

It didn't get stuck. We arrived on our still empty floor seconds later. Trent held the door open and let me step out first. I got a whiff of his cologne and had to keep myself from leaning into him and taking a deep breath. He smelled really good. Had he always smelled that good?

"Thanks again for Friday night," he said as he was about to retreat to the break room.

"Trent wait," I said after setting down my purse. "Can I ask you something?"

Trent walked towards our desks and put down his briefcase. He didn't say anything. In his regular Trent way, he just stared at me. I decided to just go ahead and ask.

"Why didn't you hit him back?" I asked finally.

He took a deep breath and let it out slowly. Was he cursing in his head? Since he didn't take out any money to add to the jar I assumed not. But I could tell there was a lot going on in his head.

"I wanted to. I really did. But you still love him and we still have to work together. There are enough people who hate me at this job. I don't need to add another."

"Whoa, whoa, whoa. Who says I still love Vinny?"

"No one has to say. You forget. I'm an expert at knowing when a woman is in love with another man." He stared into my eyes for several moments.

He was right of course. For all his faults, I still loved Vinny. I had been with him so long it was almost like I didn't know how *not* to love him.

"But trust me," Trent said still staring at me. "If that ever changes, I will gladly knock the sh -" Trent pressed his eyes shut then reached into his pocket. "You get my point," he said after dropping a dollar into his jar.

Yep, I totally got his point.

Chapter 18: Twist Out

Twist out: A style formed by untwisting hair that has been in two-strand twists for a period of time. Very effective in stretching the hair and combating shrinkage.

~~~

Hair tip #16: Try two-strand twists on dry hair in order to retain as much length as possible. After sectioning the hair, spray a little moisturizer and water, but do not saturate the hair. Twist the hair and let it dry again fully before attempting to untwist. The twists themselves can be a style for a few days before a twist out is attempted.

~~~

So, how much money do you have on you?" Carnece asked over the phone. Since she rarely called me at work, I expected this to be really important. Not an inquiry about my bank statement for a shopping trip or something.

"Do you mean on me? Or in the bank?"

"Do you think you can get your hands on like five hundred dollars in the next hour or so?"

"I guess. Why?"

"I'm in jail."

~~~

Well, this was a first. I had never had to bail someone out of jail before. I thought about letting her just stay there, but considering she was perfectly willing to help me cover up the suggested murder of my ex-boyfriend, I figured I better go help her out.

"What did you do?" I asked as we walked out of the police station.

Carnece had to pull down her too tight, too short mini skirt and practically run to keep up with me.

"Let's just say it was a bad break up."

"A break up that lands you in jail? Yeah, I'd say that's bad." I didn't know if I wanted to know the details. But as we rode in the taxi to my place I found myself beyond curious. What did she do? After a few minutes, my imagination got the better of me. "So, what -"

"I drove my car into his house," she said interrupting me.

"You what?"

"I drove my car into his house."

"Carlos? Why?"

Carnece sighed. "I thought I loved him. But the bitch that was in his bed told me I was wrong."

~~~

"Eleven kids!" Carnece said passing the merlot back to me an hour later. "I knew something was wrong with that man. No one spells James with two 'A's."

I took a sip of wine. "That's just what Trent said."

"Trent, huh?"

"Yeah, if I remember correctly, Trent assured me that anyone who spells James with two 'A's has to be a prick."

"Trent, huh?" she said again. "So, what's his story?"

"Who?"

"Don't play stupid. Trent. What's up with him?"

I shrugged. "He doesn't have a story. He's just a guy from work. I used to think he was simply an annoying jerk. Just another person at work I would not like to spend any more time with than I needed to. But he was actually turning into one of the few people at work I could tolerate. "Have you ever dated a white guy?" I don't know why I asked that. I guessed I was just curious. Vinny was my first boyfriend and he was Indian. I guess you could say I technically dated James though it was only three dates and he was black. My dating experience was admittedly limited. My limited dating experience did not include white men. That was mostly because I never had the opportunity. You would think attending a predominantly white university would give me plenty of chances, but I found my experience was quite the opposite. I had never been asked out by a white boy before. Interracial dating just didn't happen. That's not to say interracial hook ups didn't happen. Once the lights go out everybody looks the same so there were no boundaries on sex. But the romance just didn't happen.

I think that was part of the reason Vinny and I got together. Both black students and international students were marginalized at Cobalt University. When we didn't get invitations to the white mixers and frat parties, we had our own. Sometimes I honestly felt he chose me by default. There was no one else to go out with so why not me?

"Can I just say, I think it is completely hilarious that you have finally joined my world?" Carnece said.

"What do you mean?"

"The single life. It's crazy out there. And this is the first time you've ever had to actually deal with it. Vinny was your first boyfriend and he lasted almost seven years. Now you're finally getting a taste of what the dating world is really like."

"Well, I can honestly say, I don't like the flavor."

"Please, you are just getting started. Wait till you're at it for a few years. Then you will really have some stories." Carnece kicked her four inch electric blue pumps across the room and put her feet on the coffee table. "You remember the guy who asked me my shoes size on our first date?"

"No, I don't remember that," I said.

"Well, on the second date he bought me four pairs of shoes."

"Are you complaining about new shoes? You can't complain about new shoes." Seeing that my glass was empty again, I set it down and just picked up the bottle. Considering I had just bailed her out of jail, I didn't think Carnece would look down on me for drinking straight out of the bottle.

"Oh yes I can," she replied. "After dinner he took out a camera and asked me to change my shoes over and over again."

"That's so weird."

"I know right? What's even weirder is that I dated him for three more months after that!"

I almost choked on my wine. "You're kidding right?"

"He had really good taste in shoes."

Carnece and I looked at each other and burst out laughing. I wasn't sure who was crazier at that point, a man obsessed with women's shoes or the woman who dates him.

When the laughter subsided slightly, Carnece said, "And then there was the professional Scrabble player."

"How do you make a living playing Scrabble?"

"You don't. Which is why he lived with me for like two months."

"But still, a shoe fetish and a scrabble addiction doesn't quite beat eleven children,"

"Maybe not. But what about that guy who was on the Maury Povich show twice. Once because three different women claimed he was their baby daddy and then once because his two-year-old literally weighed 97 pounds."

"Maybe I don't want to do this dating thing. Maybe I should just find a way to make it work with Vinny."

"Oh, 'make it work,'" she said with air quotes. "That sounds so romantic."

"Well, I've invested a lot into that relationship. Maybe too much to let go."

"Listen to you. Maybe this. Maybe that. I may not be the best one to offer relationship advice, but I seriously think love shouldn't be about maybe. It should be a feeling so strong you can't breathe without that person."

What she said made sense. I wanted that kind of love. Which was odd because honestly, I felt I could breathe so much better without Vinny. As a matter of fact, I felt like I could breathe for the first time in my life.

Chapter 19: Cornrows

Cornrows: Underhand braids formed against the scalp.

~~~

Hair Tip #17: Be your own hair advocate. If going to a hair stylist is something you can afford and you enjoy, by all means keep doing it. But learn the truth about hair, especially your own. Don't let them talk you into styles are treatments that might be unhealthy. Seek advice, but in the end, you should know what is best for your hair.

~~~

*T*rent and I had a comfortable relationship. If you could call it a relationship. Maybe acquaintanceship would be a more appropriate word. We mostly stayed out of each other's way, but we covered for one another when needed.

"Where's Bishop?" Mr. George asked at our weekly meeting.

"Oh, um, flat tire," I said quickly. Don't know why I really said it. I had no idea whether he had a flat tire or not, but he could have. Something had to be wrong.

The truth was, Trent had left for lunch around 11 and hadn't come back. That wasn't like him. He usually never even left his desk for lunch let alone the building.

After the brief and pointless meeting in which Mr. George informed us of all the latest trends in social media, which by the way were usually already outdated and useless by the time he got to them, I went back to my desk and tried to figure out where Trent could have disappeared to.

I remembered he left right after we got our mail. I leaned over and looked at his desk. It wasn't like I was actually going to read his mail or anything, but it might give me a clue as to what happened to him. I shuffled a few of his papers on his desk but didn't see anything out of the ordinary.

Deciding I needed a closer look, I sat down and pretended to look for a pencil sharpener. As if he had a pencil sharpener. Who uses lead pencils anymore nowadays? Anyway, I looked to the left and that's when I saw something interesting next to his stapler. It was a picture of a baby. Actually, it was one of those postcards people sent out when their baby was born in order to brag to everyone. These parents didn't need to brag, however. This was one ugly baby. I almost didn't want to pick up the postcard for fear I might catch whatever red rash that baby had. But morbid curiosity made me pick it up anyway and that's when I noticed what was written on the card: Mark and April Hunt welcome Brady Hunt to the world November 15th.

April. That couldn't possibly be the April that left him at the altar. There was no possible way she would be that cold hearted as to send a baby announcement. That had to be what was wrong with Trent.

I turned the card over and noticed something else that was pretty interesting. It was a picture of Mark and April. And April was a black girl. He had dated a black girl...well had almost married a black girl. Why did I think he was racist all this time? I thought back to that conversation I had overheard. Did I hear wrong?

The rest of the afternoon ticked away slowly. Trent never returned. I had to admit, I was a bit worried about him. I wondered where he was and what he was up to. He probably went to his beach to calm down and remember how small he was in the big picture of things. Yeah, he was fine. He was at his beach.

Before I knew what I was doing, I was packing up my stuff. I wanted to find him to make sure he was okay.

No one in the office even noticed that I left as Mr. George was leading everyone in a deep breathing exercise and they all had their eyes closed. Personally, I thought the whole meditation thing was his excuse to take a nap in the middle of the day.

When I got outside of the building, I saw that Trent's car was still in the parking lot. Now I was even more worried. If his car was here and *he* wasn't then something definitely happened to him. But as I got closer to the car, I saw that he was sitting in it.

His hands gripped the steering wheel and he stared straight ahead.

"Trent? You okay?" I said, tapping on the glass. That was a stupid question. He obviously wasn't okay. The love of his life left him at the altar and then had a baby with another man less than two years later. Man that was like stabbing him, twisting the knife, and then pouring lemon juice in the wound.

He nodded, but didn't respond. I walked around to the other side and got in the passenger seat. It was freezing in the car. I wondered how long he had been sitting here.

I wasn't sure what to say to him so I just sat there staring straight ahead just like he was.

"She told me she didn't want to have kids," he said after several minutes. "I guess she meant she didn't want to have kids with *me*."

Once again I didn't know what to say. I tried to think of what Marin or Carnece would say. This time I decided to go the Carnece route. "I saw the picture. I think it's a good thing you didn't have kids with her because that is one ugly baby."

Trent slowly turned his head and looked at me. Maybe I said the wrong thing. Maybe he was still in love with her and I had just insulted her.

Trent smiled and then burst out into raucous laughter. I breathed a sigh of relief. I joined in laughing as well.

"That is so true," he said still laughing.

"His head looks like a nectarine seed," I said.

Trent laughed harder. "Thanks," he said when the laughter subsided somewhat.

"No problem," I said tightening my jacket around me. It was seriously cold in this car. "It takes one pathetic loser to comfort another pathetic loser."

Trent noticed my discomfort and started the engine. After turning on the heat he said, "Man, we are pathetic aren't we? I don't know which one of us is worse."

"Oh, come on. I totally win. I was with a guy for nearly seven years and never even met his family. I was in love with a man who was ashamed of my race."

"Are you kidding? I was publicly humiliated at my own wedding that I'm still paying for."

"Did you see that picture?" I asked. "You were saved from having ugly children. You should consider that a blessing."

"And *you* were saved from marrying a racist," he replied.

Huh. I don't think I ever thought about it that way. All this time I had thought Trent was the one who was a racist. I thought he was being nice to me lately out of some sort of charitable pity. When in fact, the man I had wanted to marry with all my heart was the one who was behaving like a bigot. We had fallen into another silence. There was something I really wanted to ask him, but didn't think I had the courage to. Finally I took a deep breath and said, "Trent can I ask you something?"

He nodded.

"Way back like a year ago or something I overheard you talking to Ray."

"Yeah," Trent said looking at me.

"You said something that I thought was ... Well, I thought you were being racist."

Trent got this look on his face that was part surprised and part confused. "What are you talking about?"

"Well, Ray was standing next to your desk and I was coming back from lunch and I distinctly remember you saying that you weren't attracted to black girls."

Trent stared into my eyes for a second. He pointed at himself. "Me? You thought *I* was racist."

I shrugged awkwardly.

Trent shook his head. "That's not what I said. In case you didn't know, my ex-fiancée is a black girl."

"Yeah, I just figured that out today."

Trent stared forward and smiled. "That's what you get for eavesdropping. That's not what I said at all."

"Well what did you say?" I asked.

"We were trying to come up with an angle for an all-girl fan club for the Baltimore Orioles. He suggested The Orange and Black Girls. I probably said something about not liking that title at all. You must have come in at the end of my sentence."

I flushed with embarrassment. A few seconds ago I was freezing and now I was so hot I could barely breathe. He wasn't even talking about race at all.

Looking at me he said, "Is that why you have always been so cold to me?"

I shrugged guiltily.

Trent shook his head. "And to think, that was right after I told Ray that I thought you were ... um ..."

"You thought I was what?"

Cornrows

Instead of answering, Trent unexpectedly put the car in gear. "Let's go," he said.

"Where are we going?" I asked buckling up. I kind of wanted to ask him to finish his thought, but I was a little afraid of what the answer would be.

"Well, if you are a true pathetic loser which I suspect you are, I know you don't have any plans so you're coming to hang out with me."

"All right. Let's do it."

~~~

Two hours later we pulled into a driveway on a quiet street in Delaware. "Where are we?" I asked.

Instead of responding, he hopped out of the car and walked around to my side. "When is the last time you had a home cooked meal?" he asked when he opened my door.

"Uh, my mother wouldn't know how to find the kitchen if you drew her a map. So I guess my answer to that is never."

"Well, you're in for a treat."

I almost had to jog to keep up with him as he strode up the front path. Without knocking, he flung open the door and said, "Ma, I'm home. Feed me!"

Ma? As in mom? We were at his parents' house?

The sound of running feet and shuffling chairs filled the air as what seemed like forty people came running to the front door.

"Trent!" several people yelled in unison. But then there was sudden silence as everyone froze and stared at me.

"Trent, aren't you going to introduce us to your friend?" A large white woman in an apron said.

Trent looked at me. And with a deadly serious face he said, "Oh, this is not a friend. She's just some homeless girl I picked up on the way over."

I punched him in the side. "Ow! Okay, everyone this is a coworker of mine. Mahogany."

My name floated over the crowd as several people repeated it as if trying it on for size. The large woman in the apron approached me. Then with a big grin she wrapped her arms around me and said, "Welcome! We are so happy to have you."

And that wasn't the only hug. I got passed around and hugged like a rag doll at least twelve more times before I somehow ended up on the couch surrounded by more of what I suspected to be Trent's family.

"I love your name," a girl seated next to me said.

"I love your hair," another girl who looked eerily similar to the first girl said. "I'm Jennifer and that's Jessica," she continued. "We're Trent's baby sisters although we're not really babies. We're juniors at Rutgers."

"Nice to meet you," I said.

"Can you do my hair like that?" Jennifer asked.

"Uh, yeah, I guess."

"Oh, my God! So awesome. I'll go get a comb." She got up and ran out of the room.

"We're sorry if we kind of mobbed you a few minutes ago," Jessica said once Jennifer was gone. "We're just so excited to meet you. You are the first girl he has brought home since..." Her sentence kind of trailed off as if she was afraid to say the name.

"April," I volunteered.

She nodded. "So you know the whole story? For months we were afraid to say her name out loud around him. He'd go into this rage. Jen and I didn't even come home for Spring Break last year because it took place during that month. But lately he's been so different. He's getting back to his old self. I bet that's because of you." She smiled as if she had a secret.

"Oh, it's not because of me. We're just coworkers."

"Right," she said nodding slowly with the same knowing smirk.

"Got it!" Jennifer said, displaying the comb like some sort of trophy. She sat down in front of me and I started my first part. Her hair was so fine I wasn't sure how they would turn out. Her long black hair was much thinner than even Vinny's. He was the last non-black person whose hair I'd braided. I don't even know why I did. I think we were just bored one night. Now that I thought about it, we were bored a lot of nights. Vinny never liked to go out and, honestly, he was never really interested in anything I was. How did we even last seven years?

~~~

"Dinner's ready!" someone called from the kitchen just as I finished the last braid.

Sitting around watching Trent's family eat dinner made me think about my own family. It was just my mother, father, John and I, but somehow we were never able to get our schedules together to share a meal. On the other hand, Trent's family was huge. There were twelve people squished together around the main dining table and then another fourteen people spread out around the house eating. Twenty six people in all. Some in college, some working in DC, some visiting from Idaho yet they all found a way to be together.

~~~

"It's getting late. I better get Mahogany home," Trent said standing. His mother had just brought out a huge pineapple upside down cake and she actually looked personally offended that he was leaving.

"You mean she's not staying for Thanksgiving?" Jennifer asked.

"Yeah, and we could use her for the big game tomorrow," Jessica added.

"What game?" I asked.

"This was just a last minute visit. I'm sure she has plans for tomorrow," Trent said.

"Actually, I don't." I reached for another roll. "My brother is in California with his in-laws. My dad is with his new family and my mom doesn't eat."

"What do you mean she doesn't eat?" Trent's dad asked.

"I mean, she doesn't eat. She's been on a diet for about thirty-five years." I could have brought up the fact that I usually spent Thanksgiving with my ex-boyfriend and that I really didn't want to be alone, but I decided to let it be.

"Well, then it's settled. Mahogany is staying the night." Trent's mom said setting down the cake in the middle of the table.

Cornrows

"I don't want to impose," I said secretly hoping they wouldn't change their mind.

"Nonsense," she said "You and Trent can stay in his old room."

Trent turned bright red. "Uh, mom. It's not like that. We're just friends."

"She can stay in our room," Jessica said. "We're going over to Tiffany's house. But first, she's got to braid my hair as well."

~~~

"Sorry about that," Trent said as he showed me upstairs to the twins' room.

"What?"

"My family. They can be kind of overwhelming. If you want to go home I can take you. Don't feel obligated to stay or anything."

"No, it's fine. I kind of like it here."

Trent smiled shyly and tried to hide it by turning away.

"Well, here's the room. Excuse the mess. My sisters are pigs. But the sheets are clean on the bed on the left. There's something for you to sleep in there," he said pointing to the top of the bed. "Uh, the bathroom is two doors down and the linen closet is next to it." Trent stood there awkwardly crossing and then uncrossing his arms. "I'm seriously sorry about this. I'll take you home any time you want. I really didn't know they'd make you stay."

"Trent, it's fine. I'm actually intrigued by this big game."

"Really? I didn't know you liked sports."

"There's a lot you don't know about me." That came out a lot more flirtatious than I expected. "Uh, good night," I said, stepping into the room and closing the door behind me.

~~~

I awoke to the smell of pancakes. I thought I was dreaming at first. I don't think I had ever woken to the smell of pancakes in my life. I stumbled down the stairs in my borrowed Tinkerbell pajamas so happy that I didn't have to fuss with my hair. The corn rows had held up nicely even without my satin cap that I usually sleep in every night.

"Wow, you're up early," Trent's mom said as I sat down at the breakfast table.

"How could anyone sleep with this glorious smell in the air?" I asked.

She smiled and set a plate of pancakes in front of me.

"Well, you ask Mr. Bishop that when he wakes up in two hours," she said with a laugh. "Coffee?"

I kind of grunted a yes as my mouth was too full of the most wonderfully, buttery, banana chocolate chip pancakes.

"Trent is already out for his morning jog."

"He jogs?"

"Yep, every morning."

"That explains it."

"Explains what?"

Crap! Did I say that out loud? I was thinking that the daily jog explained his amazing body but I sure wasn't about to say that to his mother.

"These are incredible, Mrs. Bishop," I said trying to change the subject.

"Oh call me Sheila, dear."

Sheila sat down across from me and put her hand over mine. "Can I tell you something?"

I nodded.

"I just want to thank you," she said.

"For what?"

"For what you've done for Trent. He's like a different person now."

"Sheila, I had very little to do with that," I said.

"You have a lot more to do with it than you know."

Chapter 20: Fauxhawk

Faux Hawk: A faux Mohawk is acquired in natural hair by pinning or braiding up both sides of the hair

~~~

Hair tip #18: After cornrows, you can partially unbraid the hair into a nice faux hawk. Use a moisturizer as you unbraid to give your hair a silky finish.

~~~

*T*he big game turned out to be a softball game which I was relieved about for two reasons. One, I was happy it wasn't football. I didn't want to spend the morning imagining Trent tackling me. Second of all, I made the General Motors All-Star team in softball two years in a row while I was in college. Yeah, I knew my way around a softball field. But not wanting to seem conceited, I didn't mention any of this to the Bishops before the game.

"Okay, kids," Mr. Bishop said in the dugout of the neighborhood field. "We are gonna win this year. This is *our* year."

Jennifer rolled her eyes and said, "That's what you said last year."

"And the year before. And the year before. And the year before," her twin added.

"I take it you don't win very often?" I asked.

"That's an understatement, dear," Sheila said. "We haven't beat the Bachermans in eight years."

"Yeah, and we only won that year because Angie Bacherman went into labor on the field and they had to forfeit the game," Jessica added.

"And now, eight year old Sam helps his family kick our ass each year."

"Jennifer Bishop, watch your language," her mother said.

"Well, if you lose every year why do you continue to play?" I asked.

Everyone in the family slowly turned their heads to Bob Bishop.

"What? It's tradition. We have to play," he said.

That's when the bickering started. I couldn't help but smile as twelve Bishops simultaneously complained about softball as if it was the greatest evil on the planet. It was kind of cute. Even though they were all yelling and screaming at each other, I could still tell they all really loved each other.

Trent grabbed my elbow and pulled me off to the side. "I'm really sorry about this," he said. "It's just a stupid game. You don't have to play."

"What position are you?" I asked.

"Um, short stop." He seemed surprised by my question. Did he think I didn't know my softball positions?

"I want to pitch, can I pitch?" I asked.

Once again, complete shock. "Um, Jen usually pitches."

"Are you kidding me?" Jen said out of the blue. I don't even know how she heard us over the family bickering, but somehow she did. "I only volunteer to pitch so that I have to do less running. It's all yours, Mahogany," she said handing me her glove and the ball. Then she sat down on the bench and pulled her hat over her head.

I turned to go warm up when Trent grabbed my arm again. "Is there something you're not telling me?" he asked.

"Like what?" I gave him the most innocent look I could muster, but he didn't buy it.

"You played softball in college or something didn't you?"

I nodded. "General Motors All-Star pitcher two years in a row."

Trent's lips spread into a wide, brilliant smile. It was beautiful. I was literally momentarily mesmerized by it. "Well, let's go kick some Bacherman butt, shall we?"

~~~

For some reason, the Bachermans had home field advantage even though they literally lived across the street from the Bishops. Maybe it alternated each year or maybe whoever won the year before got to be the home team. I didn't know and I didn't ask. I spent the top of the first inning studying my opponents as they fielded their positions. It was pretty easy to see who the real athletes were and who would be my biggest challenge.

Unfortunately, I didn't get long to study as their pitcher made quick work of the Bishops. They were out in seconds.

As I made my way to the mound, no one on the Bacherman team paid much attention to me. I thought I would at least get a few odd looks. I mean I was the only black girl on their team. I looked around for a second. Okay, I was the only black girl at the field. Period. But I guessed the Bachermans were so confident they were going to win that they didn't really care who was on the Bishop team. That was until I threw out my first pitch.

I had to admit that I felt like a rock star with my faux hawk as I stood on the pitcher's mound. I probably should have started out slow, but I was so excited to play that I brought the heat on the first pitch. Angie Bacherman didn't even swing. It was like she wasn't even sure what had happened.

There was a momentary silence as both the Bachermans and the Bishops stared at me in shock. Suddenly the Bacherman father burst onto the field followed by half the Bacherman clan.

"Who is this? She can't play!" he yelled. "This is a family game and she's not family."

He had a point there. I wasn't family. I hadn't even thought of that.

"She is family," Trent's dad answered. "She's Trent's girlfriend."

I started to correct him when I felt Jessica jab me in the side. "She's more than a girlfriend," Jessica added. "They're getting married."

"Well, we all know how that turned out the last time," a teenage Bacherman said with a laugh.

I glanced over at Trent. He was biting his lip so hard I think I saw a drop of blood drip out.

"Peter, you little dick," Jessica said throwing her glove at the smart mouthed kid. Then she lunged for him. Thankfully, Sheila held her back before she was able to throw a punch.

"A fiancé is not family. Not legally," Mr. Bacherman said once the fight between Carson and Jessica was under control.

"And neither is an ex-husband," Sheila said. "Or did Todd and Samantha get back together."

"She's right," Trent's dad said. "If Todd gets to play, then Mahogany gets to play."

Mr. Bacherman gritted his teeth and then stormed off the field followed by the rest of the Bacherman clan.

"Trent, you okay?" I asked as he walked past me to his position. He didn't answer at first so I grabbed his arm and said it again.

He took a deep breath and stared to where Peter was coming up to bat. Finally he said, "Let's just kill these sons of bitches."

"Well, all right then," I said. I decided not to remind him that he needed to make a deposit into his jar after that request.

~~~

Fauxhawk

'Kill them' is exactly what we did. After five innings, we hadn't let the Bacherman's score a single run. I even struck out their ringer Todd who apparently was some sort of high school star twenty years ago. In all, I had struck out eleven batters and Trent had assisted in two double plays. We were a good team. On the field, that is.

I could sense the Bacherman frustration. I felt at any moment they were going to explode or something. And at the top of the sixth, that something happened. The score was still zero to zero. They had a pretty good pitcher as well. Vivi Felton was a Bacherman cousin and she was apparently attending college on a softball scholarship just like I had done. She was definitely good, but by the sixth inning, I had her pitch figured out. As evidenced by the double I hit.

Sheila and Jessica hit after me and they both struck out. So it was up to Trent. He had gotten three hits already, but it hadn't been enough to score. This time, if he got a hit, I would be heading for home no matter what.

When Trent hit a line drive down the third base line, I took off toward home. And if we were playing a regular friendly game of softball, I would have made it easily. But since Todd was playing left field, I knew I would have to push it. I had seen how great his arm was throughout the game.

Just as I had suspected, the ball came whizzing past my head and straight to Peter at home plate. But since it wasn't a force out, he would have to tag me. I knew we needed this run so I did what any seasoned athlete would do. I barreled into home feet first and tried to avoid the tag.

Peter was so surprised that I kept running at top speed that he accidently dropped the ball. I was safe without question and the Bishops had their first run of the game.

Unfortunately, when I tried to stand up, I couldn't exactly walk anymore.

Chapter 21: Braid Out

Braid Out: Style formed by unbraiding the hair after individual braids or cornrows.

~~~

Hair tip #19: Avoid hair accessories with metal parts or anything that can snag in your hair. Not only are they painful when they get caught in your hair, but they can also cause damage.

~~~

*M*y ankle wasn't really that bad. They forget I was a college athlete. I was used to an injury here or there. But the Bishop family treated me as if my life was touch and go.

I ate Thanksgiving dinner on the couch with my foot elevated. Jen, Jess, and Trent ate on the floor in front of me in order to keep me company. And when dinner was over and everyone was exhausted, Trent carried me up to my room.

"Trent, I'm fine. I can walk," I said.

"I can't let you walk. My family would kill me. You led us to our first Bacherman victory in eight years. Isn't it obvious that they like you much better than me?" He smiled. "What kind of fiancée would I be if I let you walk on a broken ankle," he teased.

"It's not broken. Just sprained. I've had sprained ankles before. I finished the game didn't I?"

He shook his head. "I still can't believe you kept playing. If I had known..." his voice trailed off. I wondered what he would have done if I had told him.

We fell into a heightened silence as Trent reached the top of the stairs.

"You know, you're like a different person when you're with your family," I said. "I haven't seen you smile this much since the Arbor Day party."

"I was drunk out of my mind at that party."

"Yep," I said as we reached the twins' room.

We entered and Trent continued to hold me in his arms right in front of the bed. With my head against his chest, I could feel him breathing in and out and the steady rhythm of his heart.

"Are you sure I didn't slip and say anything to you that night?" he asked still holding me.

"Anything like what?" Why was he bringing this up now? I didn't want to think about how he had confessed his love to me while he was in a drunken stupor. Not now in this position. It was too freaking romantic. I was not in the mood for romantic. And, honestly, neither was he. Neither one of us was ready for romantic.

"Nothing. Never mind." He set me down gently on the bed. With his face inches from mine he whispered, "Goodnight."

Braid Out

I couldn't sleep that night. I couldn't get Trent out of my head. Trent Bishop. What in the world was happening to me? This was ridiculous. I needed a drink and not milk or tea. I needed something a bit stronger. I wondered if they had any red wine in the house. I swung my feet over the edge of the bed and stood up slowly putting weight on my ankle. It was a little painful, but not that bad. Certainly not bad enough to keep me away from a glass of wine.

As I stepped out of the bedroom, Trent came out of the bathroom. He had a towel wrapped around his waist and his hair was dripping wet.

"What are you doing?" he said in a forced whisper.

Trying not to think about what's under that towel. Thankfully, I didn't say that out loud.

"I-I … was thirsty," I stuttered.

"Wait there." He slipped into his room and emerged seconds later wearing sweatpants and holding a coke. "Here," he said, handing me the soda.

"Uh, I wasn't that kind of thirsty."

He rolled his eyes. "Fine," he said sweeping me up into his arms and whisking me down the stairs. He set me down in the recliner next to what looked like a liquor cabinet and asked me what I wanted to drink.

"Got any merlot?"

"Does my dad look like he drinks merlot? We've got brandy, gin and rum. What'll it be?"

"Brandy."

Trent poured me a glass and handed it over. Then he sat on the floor and stared up at me. "You're not having any?" I asked.

He shook his head. "I think it best I don't drink in front of you anymore."

"So you're just going to sit there and look at me?"

He turned away. "Fine, I won't look at you. I'll just wait till you finish and carry you back up the stairs."

"I told you, you don't have to do that."

"And I told you, if anything happens to you, my family will disown me and adopt you."

I smiled and sipped my Brandy. That was the cranky Trent I was used to.

"Okay, I'm done," I said a few minutes later. I felt all warm and tingly from the Brandy. It wasn't a drink I was used to and I think it had already started to affect me.

"So why were you taking a shower in the middle of the night?" I asked as he carried me up the stairs.

"Couldn't sleep."

"Why?" I asked.

He cleared his throat and said, "Couldn't get someone out of my head."

"Who?"

He paused at the top of the stairs. I could feel his heartbeat thumping faster and faster next to my ear.

Instead of answering, he set me down right outside of his sisters' bedroom.

"Goodnight, Mahogany."

He turned to walk away, but I grabbed the side of his sweatpants and pulled him back to me. "You didn't answer my question," I said. "Who can't you get out of your head?" I had a feeling I already knew the answer to that question. And from the expression on his face I could tell I was right.

Braid Out

Trent pressed his body against mine pushing me into the wall. "What are you doing, Annie?" he whispered, his breath brushing against my cheek.

I felt like my heart was throbbing in my throat. Was this really happening? When I felt his lips against mine, I knew the answer to that.

Our bodies molded into one as the kiss evolved into something deeper. I felt the kiss pulse through me as if I was getting electric shock therapy. It was a sensation I had never felt before. Definitely not with Jaames and not even with Vinny. Don't get me wrong, I used to love kissing Vinny. I loved Vinny, but this kiss was so powerful it was epic. He literally took my breath away.

Trent lifted me off the ground and I wrapped my legs around his waist. I had to stifle a moan when he moved his lips away from my mouth and to the right side of my neck. The night he got drunk I remember him saying I had a freckle on my neck that he thought was incredibly sexy. I wondered if that was the spot he was now kissing.

Somehow the door opened and we stumbled into the twins' room.

"I want you so bad, Annie," he said as he set me on the bed. Something about the way he called me Annie excited me more than I expected. Maybe it was the fact that he was the only one in the world who called me that.

I reached under his shirt and felt those abs that I had begun to crave. Trent leaned up and whipped off his t-shirt. My God he was sexy. And the way he kissed me made me want to scream out in ecstasy. If I knew he could kiss like this I would have been doing this a long time ago.

"Vinny," I said. I don't know why I said that I don't know how I could confuse Trent for Vinny. They were nothing alike. Maybe it was the fact that I actually felt kind of guilty. After seven years with Vinny, he had never made me feel the way Trent had in about thirty-five seconds.

Trent froze. Literally. I felt his skin turn cold. He climbed off the bed and silently picked up his shirt.

"Trent. I'm sorry," I said knowing that a simple apology was not going to be enough. Trent had been left at the altar for another man and I had just called him by my ex-boyfriend's name. What a way to kill the moment.

"I...Uh...I'm gonna go." He turned toward the door. "I'll take you home in the morning."

"Trent, wait." But he didn't. He walked out of the door without another word.

~~~

Having cornrows in my hair for a few days led to a great braid out. I took my time in the morning unbraiding my hair and finger combing it into a nice crinkly fro. My hair looked incredible but I felt like crap. How could I do this to Trent? It wasn't like I even wanted Vinny anymore. That was something the last few days had shown me. And one kiss from Trent had confirmed it. I was in love with Trent Bishop. I had to fix this. Unfortunately, I had no idea how.

Chapter 22: Banded

Banding: A method used to stretch the hair that often works better than braids or twists. Section the hair, and a rubber band close to the scalp. Pull the hair straight as you add more bands all the way down the hair to the ends.

~~~

Hair tip #20: When trying this process, make sure to use the bands without the metal clip so it won't pull out your hair when you take them out in the morning.

~~~

*T*rent wasn't there the next morning. Apparently he had left before dawn to go for a jog and hadn't returned. By three o'clock that afternoon Jessica offered to drive me back to DC.

"So, did you and my brother have a fight?" she asked during the trip.

"I think so."

She was quiet for several minutes. I could tell she wanted to say something; she just wasn't sure how to phrase it.

"If you're not sure about him, if there is any doubt in your mind, please leave him alone. I don't think he could handle another bad break up."

"What happened to him after April?" I asked suddenly curious about the details. I never asked Trent before. I assumed it was bad, but the tone in Jessica's voice made me feel like it was something beyond bad.

"Trent used to be the sweetest most fun-loving guy ever. April took all of that away. He was like a different person after. He disappeared for two months. We didn't hear from him for two whole months. We didn't know if he was dead or alive. It was the scariest time in our lives. Turns out he had backpacked through the Andes Mountains. When he finally showed back up, he was this bitter, angry monster. Two days ago, when he walked through the door with you, was the first time we got a glimpse of the pre-April Trent. If you're not the one, if you can't be what he needs, please just end it now."

"I'm not sure if we ever really had anything. But if we did, I think I successfully ended it last night."

"Is that what you want?" she asked.

I couldn't answer that. How could I give her an answer when I wasn't sure myself? It was too much pressure.

"Can I ask you something?" I said after a few minutes.

Jessica shrugged.

"This might sound odd, but I was just wondering how your family feels about the whole race thing."

Jessica looked confused. "What race thing? Dog races? Is he gambling again? Oh Daddy is going to kill him."

"No, he's not gambling, I don't think." Gambling? So he had a gambling addiction as well? Huh? I shook my head and continued, "I was talking about my race."

"Why would that be a problem? You know April was black, right? Look, Trent definitely has a type if you know what I mean. Let's just say his first crush was TBoz from TLC."

I had to hold in a smile as I imagined a young Trent drooling at the television while grooving to "Waterfalls."

"Look, Mahogany. I know I don't know you very well, but I can already see what he sees in you. I just want my brother to be happy. Please don't let him run away from it."

~~~

I spent the weekend locked in my apartment thinking about Vinny and Trent. Funny how James with two 'A's never even entered the equation. I called the Bishop house a few times, but Trent was never there. I could tell his family was afraid he had pulled another disappearing act. After a little investigation, I found out where he lived in DC and went to find him. He wasn't there. And for someone who worked for a social media firm, he was extremely difficult to find through, well, social media. He didn't have a Facebook account, he wasn't on Twitter, and Googling his name only brought up some thick-necked rugby player.

At work, it was Trent's turn to take off for a few days. After I broke up with Vinny, I didn't come to work for almost a week. After our disastrous Thanksgiving, Trent didn't show up for three days.

To keep my mind off of him, I focused on my hair. Yes, I had become slightly obsessed with my hair, but it was the only thing that helped me get through my man troubles. Through countless YouTube video searches, I discovered a technique called banding. It was a way to stretch the hair so that it looked closer to its actual length. I always hated how my hair could be like six inches long but only appear to be like two due to the curl pattern. This technique which involved using multiple rubber bands along small sections of hair made so much sense. After banding, my hair looked almost as long as it did after flat ironing, but without using the heat. With the rubber bands in my hair, I looked like a girl from an African art painting I had seen before. I wondered if this was what my ancestors in Africa had done to their hair to make it longer and more manageable. Maybe it was something that was lost during the centuries black people were forced into slavery. A tradition that didn't survive the boat ride. For centuries black people were forced to make do using products and styles that weren't suited to their hair type.

~~~

Finally, on the following Thursday, I came in early to find Trent seated at his desk.

"Hey," I said, approaching him.

"Hey," he said without taking his eyes off of the computer screen.

"I was worried about you."

"Why?" he said coldly.

"Because ..." he was not going to make this easy for me. "Look, Trent, I know I messed up, but can you let me try to explain?"

I took his lack of response as a cue to continue. "I'm not in love with Vinny anymore. I'm over him. I am. But I was with him for seven years. He was the only man I had ever been attracted to, the only man I had ever been ... intimate with. That was until you. Oddly enough, even after everything he has put me through; I think I still feel guilty for what I feel for you."

Trent still didn't respond. He didn't even look at me. I dropped my stuff and spun his chair around so that he was looking directly at me. "Do you understand what I'm trying to tell you? Trent, I love you."

He closed his eyes and turned away. After taking a deep breath he said, "I think it's best if we just have a professional relationship."

I wasn't letting him off that easy. "Best for whom? You? Because you're too scared to give love a chance."

"Damn right I'm scared. I did the love thing once and it didn't work out too well, did it? I almost fell for it again. I almost opened myself up to you just so it could happen again."

"It won't happen again. I'm not April!"

"And I'm not Vinny!" He stood up forcing me to step back.

We started a staring match. Neither one of us wanted to be the first to back down.

"I've got work to do," he said sitting.

I knew there was something between us. I had a connection with Trent that I hadn't ever had with anyone.

But maybe it was the wrong timing. We were both mending our wounds from our last relationships. It might be best to wait until we worked out all of our personal issues before we tried a relationship. Of course, after calling him Vinny in the heat of passion, he might never, ever want a relationship with me.

I sat down at my desk with a lump in my throat. I didn't want to cry. I didn't want to run and hide in the bathroom and give in to tears. I didn't want him to see me like that. He had already seen me at my worst. I wanted to save face and show that I could be just as cold and uncaring as him sitting over at his desk coding another website.

I think at least two hours passed without either of us moving from our seats. It was almost as if we were having our own secret little competition to see who could be the most productive and show they were the least emotional. Whisperings around the office, however, brought me out of my working trance. I could instantly tell that something was going on. I looked up and realized what it was. Vinny. He was standing in the middle of the bean bag circle wearing a tux and holding a dozen roses.

What the hell? Why now?

I stole a quick glance at Trent. Of course, he kept his eyes glued to his computer screen and pretended he didn't see what was happening.

"Vinny? What are you doing here?"

"I'm doing something I should have done a long time ago," he said taking out a small box that could only possibly hold an engagement ring. The women in the

office gasped as if they were personally witnessing their
own corny romantic movie.

"Vinny, please."

"No, Mags, listen. I love you and I want to be with
you. These past eight months have been absolutely
miserable for me. If the only way I can get you to come
back is to marry you, then I want to marry you."

Wait. Did he just say he wanted to marry me so that
I would come back to him? Not quite the proposal I was
looking for. It was like he was offering to marry me as a
last resort. The only way he could get me back. This was
no way to start a marriage.

I glanced over at Trent as he coughed into his fist. I
knew he hadn't suddenly gotten a tickle in his throat. He
was giving his own personal commentary about the way
Vinny had just proposed.

"Are you serious?" I asked Vinny.

"Yes, I'm serious. I want to marry you." He took the
gold band out of the box and held it up for everyone to
see as if he had to prove something.

I pressed my eyes shut and rubbed my temples. He
didn't have a clue that anything was wrong with what he
had just said.

"Let's go talk about this," I said grabbing his hand
and leading him into the hallway.

"I don't understand," Vinny said once we were out
of the office. "Isn't this what you wanted? We can get
married."

"Vinny, come on. This is not how I want it. I don't
want you traipsing into my place of work announcing to
everyone that you're marrying me as a last resort."

"That's not what I said and you know it."

"You said if it's the only way to get me back you'll marry me. Not exactly romantic."

Vinny threw the flowers against the wall. "I don't know what you want from me, Maggie. What the hell is going on with you? Why can't you just be happy?"

"You're right. I can be happy. But I can't be happy with you. Not anymore."

"So that's it?" he asked.

"Yeah, that's it." I turned to go back into my office, but he grabbed my arm.

"You're insane, Maggie. Think about this. You're not going to get anyone else."

"And what exactly is that supposed to mean?" He just went from proposing to me to really pissing me off in about three seconds.

"What I mean is that men aren't exactly beating down your door."

"Listen to me, Vinyay Gupta. I'm not sure what I ever saw in you, but let me assure you, my vision has cleared. You are a selfish, petty, and immature little boy and I want nothing to do with you."

Before I could retreat into the office, Trent came out. "You heard her," he said. "Just get out of here."

Vinny looked back and forth between the two of us. "So there *is* something between you two."

"That's none of your business," I said.

"It *is* my business. You lied to me. What did I do to deserve that?"

"You treated her like she wasn't good enough for almost seven years," Trent volunteered. "That's what you did."

"Stay out of this," Vinny said taking a swing at Trent.

Trent dodged left then landed an uppercut to Vinny's chin. Vinny fell backwards and slid against the wall to the ground. He tried to stand but couldn't quite get his bearings. Meanwhile, Trent calmly walked over to the elevator and pushed the button. When the doors opened, he picked up Vinny and tossed him inside as if he weighed no more than a bag of SunChips.

Then without saying a word, he straightened his tie and calmly walked back into the office.

Chapter 23: Baby Hair

Baby hair: When black babies are born, they all have this soft curly hair. For most of the children, their hair texture changes into a coarse kinky texture sometime during childhood. I have talked to several people who wished they could always have this 'baby hair.' I even saw a documentary about the Dominican Republic that said some women rub placenta on their baby's heads in hopes to keep the soft texture. Gross. But that got me thinking, what is different for those babies than for us adults. Well, their heads are completely submerged in liquid twenty four hours a day for nine months. So we, too, need to keep our hair as moisturized as possible as often as possible. Water is good for your hair. Don't run from it!

~~~

Hair tip #21: Carry a small bottle of water around with you in your purse. Give your hair a spritz throughout the day in order to keep it moist.

~~~

Baby Hair

*M*arin is having the baby," John said over the phone. He should have sounded ecstatic. He was about to have his first child. But instead he sounded small and scared.

"What's wrong?" I threw the covers off the bed and sat up.

"There was so much blood." His voice cracked when he said the word blood. "Marin passed out. I didn't know what to do."

"Oh my God. John, it's okay. She's going to be fine." Why do people always say that when in truth they have absolutely no idea if it will be fine or not? I started getting dressed with one hand while still holding the phone to my ear. "Do Mom and Dad know?" I asked.

"You're the first person I called," he said.

"John, I'm coming. I'll call them when I get in the car."

~~~

John was sitting in the waiting room with his head in his hands when I arrived. "How is she?" I asked.

As soon as he looked at me, the tears began. Unable to respond, he buried his head into my shoulder and kept crying. "John, what happened? Is Marin okay? What about the baby?"

He pulled away and wiped his tears. "The baby is fine. Marin's not. She's in surgery. I don't know if she's going to make it. What am I going to do if she doesn't make it?"

"Don't talk like that," I said hugging him again. "We're not going to lose her." Suddenly I became a cheerleader trying to keep him from succumbing to despair. "Come on, let's go see the baby."

~~~

"What are you going to name him?" I asked holding my nephew in my arms.

"What? Oh, I don't know," he said. He seemed so distracted. "Marin had some ideas. I can't really remember what they are right now."

"Do you want to hold him?"

He shook his head.

I felt so bad for him. He was unshaven, his shirt was untucked and he wasn't even wearing a tie. I don't think I had seen him without a tie since he was a senior in high school. One day senior year he decided he felt better in a suit and so he wore one every day even when he was in school. Everyone thought he was insane, but he didn't care. That's just the way he was. Straight laced, predictable, and well, completely boring. So four years ago when he came back from a business trip in Phoenix, Arizona with a wife, to say we were shocked is an understatement.

"You really love her don't you?" I asked.

He looked at me strangely then. As if I was an alien or something.

"Sorry, that was a stupid question," I said. I placed the baby in the bassinet next to what would be Marin's bed if she ever got out of surgery. "Tell me about the night you met. How did you know she was the one?"

John shrugged and looked out of the window. "Everyone thinks we're so different," he said. "But really,

I think we're exactly the same. I think that's what I love about her. She's me without being ... me."

She's me without being me. Those words repeated in my head over and over again. That's the feeling I wanted. And I realized that was a feeling I would never have with Vinny. We got together seven years ago kind of by default. We were two brown people in a white school who couldn't get dates with anyone else. So we dated each other. I think love might have come in to play later, but it wasn't there immediately.

"Mr. Brown?" a doctor asked stepping into the room.

"How is she?" Instead of responding to John, he looked over at me. "It's okay. She's my sister. You can talk in front of her."

The doctor took a deep breath. "She made it through surgery fine. She is on her way out."

"So what happened to her? What did you do?" my brother asked.

"We had to do an emergency hysterectomy. I'm sorry, she won't be able to have any more children."

John sighed. "As long as she's all right."

"She's fine," the doctor said slapping John on the shoulder.

After the doctor left, my brother walked over to the bassinet and picked up his son. "She's okay," he whispered to him. "Mommy's okay."

~~~

"What are you thinking about?" Marin asked two days later. She was still in the hospital and I didn't want to leave her there. Not at the mercy of my parents. Both of them had stuck their noses into the health of Marin and the baby so much that even *I* wanted to kick them out and ban them from the hospital. They even wanted to name the baby. Thankfully, John put a stop to that immediately. If left up to my dad, the baby would be called something boring and predictable like John and if left up to my mother the baby would be named after an inanimate object like Mahogany. Both were unacceptable to him. The constant fighting would have driven a normal person insane especially just after having surgery, but Marin just bore it all with a smile. She really was like some sort of saint.

I shrugged in response to her question.

"You're thinking of him aren't you?"

I looked at her. From the gleam in her eyes I knew she was thinking romance. "No, I'm not thinking of Vinny."

"Well, that's obvious. You're thinking of the dirty cop, aren't you?"

"What?"

"From the party. The costume Arbor Day party."

"Oh, you mean Trent." I pressed my eyes shut. Yeah, I was thinking about him, but that was pointless. Absolutely pointless. I didn't know if he'd ever forgive me for what I did.

"You want to talk about it?" she asked.

I shook my head. "You have your own problems. You don't need to hear about my love life."

"Oh, so now it's love, huh?"

"I didn't...I mean..."

"Just get over here and tell me all about it," she said patting a space next to her on the bed.

~~~

"So how do you know he hasn't forgiven you?" she asked after I gave her all the details.

"I can see it in his eyes. He wants nothing to do with me."

"Of course he does," she said.

"How do you know?"

"Trust me. He knows you love him and not Vinny."

"How in the world did you come to that conclusion after what I just told you?"

"Did he or did he not punch Vinny in the face at your office?"

"He did."

"And what did he tell you the last time he had the opportunity to punch him but didn't?"

I thought back to that day after the costume party. Vinny had sucker punched Trent right in the face. At work when I asked him why he didn't punch back, Trent said it was because I still loved Vinny. At that point I did. But he also said that when he knew I didn't love Vinny any more, he'd punch him for sure. I guess Vinny's black eye was proof that Trent knew I was over Vinny. So what? I still didn't know if that was enough for him to forgive me for calling him the wrong name in the heat of passion.

"So let's summarize," Marin said picking up her baby. "He tells you he loves you, and you don't believe him. Then you tell him you love him and he doesn't believe you."

"It's not exactly like that. He was drunk he didn't know what he was saying."

Marin shook her head. "You two are exactly alike."

"What?"

"Did I stutter? You two are alike. You are him and he is you. It's as simple as that."

John said something like that. He said he knew he wanted to marry Marin because she was him without being him. It was a beautiful sentiment and I don't think I understood it until that moment.

Chapter 24: Blow out

Blow Out: This is probably one of the most damaging ways to stretch your hair. Basically, you take a blow drier with a comb and blow your hair partially straight. It's damaging but it makes your afro look huge and amazing. Just don't do it too often.

~~~

Hair tip #22: It might seem ridiculous, but celebrate your hair. It's unique, it's beautiful, it's you.

~~~

A part of me already knew that Trent was the one for me, but I think I wasn't completely convinced until after I had spoken to Marin. That was when I decided I couldn't live without him and that I was going to fight for him. And it wasn't like I'd have to literally fight some chick for him. I just had to fight my own stupid comments and Trent's stubbornness. Now that I thought about it, it might be easier to fight another girl for him.

As soon as Marin, John and the baby were settled at home, I jumped in my car and drove back to DC. I had to see him. I had to let him know that we should be together and that I would never hurt him ...well, never hurt him again that is. I think I had already done a pretty good job of hurting him the first time.

On the way, I stopped at the little piece of beach that he loved and picked up a little souvenir. I had it all planned out. It was going to be so sweet and romantic. The fairy-tale ending that deep down we both wanted. I filled a ring box with sand from his beach. I planned on handing it to him and saying, "Let's be small together." Romantic, right? It took me the entire five hour trip to come up with that line. Unfortunately, I didn't get an opportunity to use it.

Trent wasn't at his apartment. In fact, no one was. It was completely empty. Before I panicked, I headed to the office. Maybe he just moved. Yeah, he just decided to move and didn't want me to know his new address. Of course, him picking up and moving without telling me didn't bode well for my plan. Maybe Marin was wrong and he didn't love me at all.

Instead of falling into full on panic mode, I headed to work. It was three o'clock on a Tuesday. He was sure to be there. I would do my sand line there in front of everyone. I didn't care who knew it. I loved Trent Bishop and I didn't care who knew.

As soon as the elevator opened to our floor, I knew something was wrong. I entered our office and stood in the middle of the bean bag circle as everyone was sitting on the floor meditating or napping or whatever it was they did and I stared at the desk. The one lone desk. *My* desk. Trent's desk was gone.

Blow Out

"Mr. George!" I called as I stepped over a few bodies and headed toward him. "Mr. George, where is Trent's desk? Where is Trent?"

"Mahogany, this is a quiet zone right now. You are disturbing the peaceful energy," he said with his eyes closed.

I bit my lip to keep from saying anything vulgar. Maybe I needed a jar like Trent's.

"Have a seat and I'll tell you about Trent," Mr. George added in a calming whisper.

I was not looking forward to squatting on the floor especially in the skirt I was wearing, but I really wanted to know what had happened to him.

"Trent asked for a three month vacation in order to go on a soul searching journey," Mr. George said after I had carefully maneuvered myself into a seated position.

"Three months? You gave him three months' vacation to go find his soul? Well, where the hell did it go? Timbuktu?"

"Actually, Nepal."

Nepal? He had up and gone to Nepal. Just like that.

"Well, I think I need to find my soul as well. Can I have three months off, too?" I asked.

"I hear the mocking tone in your voice, Mahogany. You don't take this seriously so you cannot have three months off." He took a deep breath and then opened his eyes. "Besides, I need you to maintain his websites until we hire a replacement."

Wow, I really needed that jar.

So, he was gone and so was my chance at a big romantic gesture that led to a happily ever after. Maybe there was no happily ever after for me.

~~~

Vinny, James with two 'A's, and Trent. Those were the only three men who had been in my life. Pathetic. And I can't even really say I dated Trent. Yeah I was completely in love with him, but we had never actually been on a date. So really you could say that I was twenty-eight and had only dated two men. That's even more pathetic.

Deciding that maybe I needed to work on me for a while, I refused to even look at men for the next few months. Seriously, I would even change the channel when those men's body wash commercials came on. Instead, I focused on my hair. That was the plan to begin with, wasn't it? I was going to focus on my hair so that I wouldn't think about Vinny. Well, now I was going to focus on my hair to avoid thinking about Trent.

Before I knew it, it was time for my one year hair birthday. Don't mock me. It's really a thing and it is really a cause for celebration. I had gone an entire year with natural hair. Though tempted, I didn't give up. I didn't revert back to a relaxer, I didn't chop it all off again out of frustration, I didn't even feel the need to get a wig, weave or extensions to ride out the rough days. I stuck it out and that meant a lot. Even on the days when I knew my hair wasn't fly, I held my head up and walked with pride. Yes, it was hard at times, but I did it. It showed me that I was stronger than I thought. This year of natural hair taught me that I had all the confidence in myself that

I needed in order to not let myself be defined by said natural hair.

As part of my hair birthday celebration, I bought myself a cake and a party hat. Not a dinky little paper hat. I'm talking a really nice Flora Bella Raffia Fedora. After sticking with me for an entire year, my hair deserved the best. Then I did an epic blowout. My hair was huge. I took out a ruler and happily did a length check. One thing I learned over the past year was that different parts of your hair grow at different rates. I think the same can be said about people as well. Different parts of your personality grow and change at different rates. Anyway, at the longest part of my hair which for me was in the top center of my head, my hair measured eleven inches when stretched out. Eleven inches! That meant it had grown almost eight inches in a year. I was so happy that I decided it was time for cake.

Just as I set the cake on the table, I heard a knock on the door.

I didn't recognize the figure in front of me at first. He had a scraggily beard and was dressed kind of like a male version of Marin. That's to say like a hippie. Finally the electric blue eyes struck me. "Trent?"

"Hi, Annie." The sound of his voice calling me Annie almost made me melt into a puddle on the spot. But somehow I kept my composure.

"Um. Hi." A knot developed in my throat. I felt tears welling in my eyes. I couldn't believe how happy I was to see him. I took some slow calming breaths and tried to swallow my emotions.

"Can I come in?"

"Oh, yeah, yeah, come in," I said stepping aside.

"Sorry for my appearance," he said as he set down a large backpack. "I literally just got off a plane from Kathmandu."

"Kathmandu? So you really did go to Nepal?"

"Yeah, where did you think I was?" he asked.

"How was I supposed to know? You just up and left. No note, no phone call, your family didn't even know how to get in contact with you."

Trent rubbed the back of his neck and looked toward the ground guiltily.

"Yeah, that probably wasn't too cool of me," he said.

"Ya think?"

He smiled. Even through that nasty scraggily beard I recognized his beautiful smile.

"Hey, can I use your bathroom?" he asked.

"You know where it is," I said trying to sound cool and in control.

Trent spent so long in the bathroom that I thought he might have tripped, hit his head and died or something. Seriously, I was starting to get freaked out, but when he emerged I saw why.

"I hope you didn't use my Venus razor on your face. I just bought that."

He froze for a second. "I'm sorry, I didn't know it -"

"I'm just kidding. It's fine." I had to resist the urge to say *he* was fine. But he really did look amazing with his freshly shaven face.

I didn't realize we were frozen and staring at each other until he broke the silence and said, "So whose birthday is it?"

"What?" I asked.

Pointing to the cake behind me he said, "Who's celebrating?"

"Oh, my hair." Yeah, I didn't realize how ridiculous that sounded until I said it out loud to him. No wonder I didn't invite Carnece or Marin. I think I would have felt better if I had said my cat ... even though I didn't have a cat.

"So you just got off a plane and you came straight here?" I asked partly because I was curious, but mostly because I wanted to take the attention off the fact that I was having a birthday party for my hair.

He rubbed the back of his neck again and turned away. Looking out of the window he said, "I ran. I ran from us and I ran from what we could have been because I was scared. That's what this whole climbing Everest thing was about."

"Wait a minute. You climbed Everest?"

He turned to me and nodded. "And let me tell you something, climbing the highest mountain in the world wasn't enough to get you off my mind."

My heart accelerated. I thought sure he'd be able to see it pounding through my clothes. But if he did, he didn't let on as he crossed the room and took my hands in his. "So, as soon as I got back in this time zone, the first thing I wanted to do was see you and tell you that I love you, Mahogany Michelle Brown."

I took another deep breath and tried to calm my nerves. This was my chance. I still had the ring box with the sand. I was finally going to get a chance to say it.

"I have something for you. Wait here." I rushed to my room, grabbed the box and came back. "I wanted to do this three months ago, but you disappeared." I cleared my throat and started the speech I had prepared. "Trent Bishop, you challenge me in ways I never thought I'd enjoy. You make me see things I've never noticed before. You give me feelings I can't even describe, but I know one of those feelings is love. I love you, Trent." I opened the box and said, "Let's be small together."

He flashed his brilliant smile and said, "How long did it take you to come up with that little speech?"

"Like two days. And then I had three months to perfect it. Was it good? Did you like it?"

He nodded. "It was perfect. Just like you."

Perfect? He thought I was perfect. Either he was blind and stupid, or he had just summed up what love really was. It's not really about being perfect in general. It was more about being perfect for one person in particular. That's what Trent and I were.

I think the whole seven years I was with Vinny, I was trying to be something I wasn't. But with Trent I could just be me. I can't believe it took me so long to figure that out. It's amazing how much you can grow in a year.

About the Author

Leslie DuBois lives in Charleston, South Carolina with her husband and two children. She currently attends the Medical University where she's earning her PhD in Biostatistics. Leslie enjoys writing stories and novels that integrate races. Her other novels include Ain't No Sunshine, Nobody Girl, Shadows of St. Louis, The Dancing Dream Series, Guardian of Eden and Nothing Else Matters.

Read an excerpt from another Contemporary Fiction Novel from Leslie DuBois

Nobody
Girl

Prologue

Sex was so much better when he paid for it. Maybe the knowledge that he could use his money to get whatever he wanted somehow added to the excitement. No matter who it was, everyone had a price. And the types of girls he wanted were quite expensive, but supremely worth it.

Tonight was going to be one of his best. Amanda had finally found him a virgin. It had been months since his last one. He loved the challenge of virgins. He had perfected an excellent combination of enhancement drugs and alcohol that gave them the optimal amount of pliability.

He wore only a towel as he sat next to her and stroked her long brown hair, waiting for the drugs to kick in. It worked quickly. Much quicker than the last girl. Within seconds, she had started removing her sweater, complaining that she was hot. This girl definitely could not hold her liquor.

"How would you like to take a bath with me? It will help you relax," he asked.

"Okay," she giggled.

He stood and went to the bathroom to run the water. This would work out perfectly. They would sit together naked in a warm bath becoming more and more aroused by the touch of each other's skin, then make love repeatedly in every room of the suite.

He slipped off his towel then walked to the bed to find her passed out. He lifted her arm and tapped her cheek, but she was out cold. This wouldn't do. He wanted a willing participant, not this. He was too good for rape.

He sat next to the passed out teenager on his bed, stroked her hair and whispered in her ear hoping to awaken her, but she didn't move.

It was getting late. He needed to get home to his wife.

He felt for her pulse. It was really weak. Too weak. What if he had given her too much of the concoction? His pulse quickened. He couldn't deal with a dead girl. He picked up his phone and called his bodyguard. He would know how to handle this situation discreetly.

Chapter 1

Delia stood in the center of her living room clutching her carry-on to her stomach like a nervous child about to be punished. She'd tried waiting for her husband on the lush leather couch, but it didn't feel natural. She hated that couch anyway. She hadn't used it since she caught Jason making out with Maria on it a year ago. Why she didn't leave him then was a mystery to her.

She looked at the gold and ivory grandfather clock that stood next to the archway separating the living room from the formal dining room to make sure the time matched what her watch said. He should have been home hours ago.

Delia grabbed a tissue out of the pocket of her jeans and sneezed into it as she wondered what his excuse would be this time. "Baby, I'm sorry I had to work late. Didn't you get my message?" "Baby, I had a flat tire and my cell phone died." "Baby, I saw an injured puppy on the side of the road and I just had to help it." "Baby, that's not lipstick on my collar, it's … it's tomato soup!"

Sure, those lines sounded stupid now, but they'd worked in the past. There was just something about Jason James she couldn't resist. Something about his sensual brown eyes and luscious lips made him like air to her. He was irresistible. She needed him, his touch, his reassurance to feel whole. The problem was he also seemed irresistible to Maria, Patricia, Claudia, Vanessa and Linda. Either that man was a nymphomaniac or he couldn't resist women whose names ended with 'a.'

Delia dropped her bag next to the rest of her luggage and began pacing the marble floor. The longer time ticked on, the more her resolve waned. She sneezed three times into her tissue. She always sneezed when she was nervous. And what could make her more nervous than the idea of completely restarting her life?

Could she really walk out on her marriage? Could she really leave Jason, the only man she'd ever been with? The catch of George Washington University. The man that all the girls wanted. He had chosen her. Out of all the women he could have had, he'd chosen her to marry. Maybe he really did love her. Maybe they could go to counseling. Yeah, she could make it work.

Just as Delia was about to drag her luggage back toward the bedroom, the phone rang.

"Did he come home yet?" Donna Lee asked without a 'hello.'

"Look, I've been thinking. Maybe I just didn't work hard enough at our marriage. Maybe we could get counseling and be happy ... "

"Dee, don't wimp out on me now. Jason is a dog and he will never change. We've been through this before, okay? Just because he looks like Johnny Depp and has more money than Oprah doesn't give him the right to treat you any way he wants. How long are you going to let him play you? He's eating away at your self-esteem. You need to get away from him before there is nothing left."

Chapter 1

Deep down, Delia knew her sister was right, but she didn't want to be a failure anymore. She wanted to be a better person and wife. The type of wife that could keep her husband satisfied.

Delia wandered into Jason's dressing room. It was identical to hers, found on the other side of the bedroom, except that Jason had added a few extra features. Besides the wall-to-wall mirrors, he had special compartments for his shoes that slid from the walls at the press of a button, and a rotating closet. He'd offered to make the same upgrades in her room, but she didn't see the need. She didn't own half as many clothes as he did.

Staring at her reflection in one of the many mirrors, she twisted a lock of hair around her finger and listened to her sister ramble off the reasons why she needed to leave Jason. She was beautiful once. At least that was what Jason told her four years ago as he stared into her green eyes and stroked her dark curly hair on their first date. She had been a senior in college and had never even been on a date, being too busy trying to finish her math, computer science, and physics triple major.

In a matter of hours, she was madly in love. She thought he would dump her the moment he found out she wouldn't sleep with him until they were married, but instead he married her. They eloped graduation night, making Delia possibly the happiest co-ed on campus. But her bliss had been short-lived as she began to realize that Jason had wandering eyes ... and hands ... and other body parts.

As she looked in the mirror, she focused on her eyes and the bags that had begun to develop underneath them. Bags that came from the countless sleepless nights of wondering where her husband was and whom he was with. She didn't cry anymore over it. She'd given up crying about two years ago. It did no good. Delia reached for her purse and began applying some foundation, the new Queen Latifah brand for dark sisters. Maybe if she were prettier, she could be enough for him.

"Are you listening to me, Dee?"

"What? Huh? Yeah, um, I think I'm gonna give it one more shot. I mean he's the love of my life. I can't just give up on us."

Donna Lee sighed on the other end of the phone.

"That's it! I'm coming over and dragging you out of that million dollar nightmare myself."

"Donna Lee don't. I'm fine really. I can make it work."

"But that's just it, Dee. You don't have to make it work. You don't have to live like this. I know you don't believe me, but you deserve better."

Delia didn't respond.

"This all goes back to being adopted, doesn't it? I was adopted, too, you know. You don't see me settling for scumbags like Jason. I wish Mom had never told you about your biological parents."

Tears welled in her eyes as she thought about her parents. She always knew she was adopted, being that she was black, her sister was Korean, and her little brother was Hispanic, but it wasn't until she was in high school that being adopted really affected her. That was when her mother, Jolie, told her that she was found in a dumpster at four months old.

She would've felt better about the situation if her biological parents had realized they couldn't take care of her and taken her to an adoption agency or children's home. But, instead, after caring for her for four months, they realized she wasn't worth anything and threw her out like trash, like she was a nobody.

Jason didn't think she was trash. He had married her. He had to love her at some point. And that was enough for her.

After hanging up with her sister, she put her luggage into her dressing room so Jason would never know she'd

Chapter 1

considered leaving. She eyed a black see-through nightie that she hadn't worn in years and considered surprising him with it as he opened the door. No, she thought, we need to talk first.

She looked at the clock over the bed they rarely shared together. Nine-thirty. Even though Jason got off work at five, he usually didn't come home until ten. If she hurried, she could make a nice spread on the dinner table using the leftovers from last night.

Last night. The night that should have been their four-year wedding anniversary. The night that had turned into the final straw. Delia spent the day preparing his favorite meal, lighting candles and covering the house with rose petals, only to have Jason not show up. At eleven, Delia blew out the candles and put the food away. Then she climbed into bed sullen and empty. She couldn't even eat the rack of lamb, rosemary potatoes, and strawberry soufflé she'd slaved over.

Sometime during the night, Jason crawled into bed next to her and wrapped her in his strong arms. She should have kicked him out then and there, but instead, she pretended she was asleep and nestled herself further into his warm, masculine body. She pretended they were still in love even though he smelled of women's perfume.

The morning after the failed anniversary surprise, Donna Lee came over and helped Delia pack her bags, trying to convince her to leave immediately. But Delia wanted to stay and at least give him an explanation. Not that he had ever bestowed upon her the same courtesy.

After setting the table … again, and lighting the candles … again, she reconsidered the nightie. Maybe that's what they needed to rekindle their relationship. He always wanted her to explore her sexuality more. She was always much too shy and timid to try the games he wanted to play in the bedroom. The occasional dirty movie and slinky lingerie was as far as she would go. Maybe that's why he found it necessary to go elsewhere. Yes, the nightie was what she needed. The nightie was the key.

As she slipped the silk nightgown off the hanger, her cell phone rang again. This time it was Jason.

"Hey, Baby, sorry I'm late. I had to help out a friend." His voice sounded tired and far away, yet still sexy as ever.

"It's okay. When will you be home?" Her voice sounded hopeful to the point of desperate and she hated that but didn't know how to change it.

"Actually, I'm turning on to our street as we speak. I'll be up in a minute."

Delia clicked off the phone then hurriedly undressed. She slipped on the nightie, dabbed on some perfume then dashed to the living room in order to see his face when he opened the door. She caught a glimpse of herself in the mirror above the couch. She looked good, really good. Large chest, delicate waist, and firm behind. She stared at her oversized breasts for a moment. They were a wedding gift from Jason. She never thought anything was wrong with her size before, but he had insisted that going two sizes larger would make her feel better about herself. In reality, they just made Jason feel better about her. All she got out of them were painful shoulder indentations from piercing bra straps.

As she heard Jason's key turn in the door knob, her heart began to race. What if he laughed at her? What if her body wasn't up to his standards anymore? But the look on his face when he got a glimpse of her told her that wasn't the case.

"Wow!" he said, putting down his briefcase. "You look amazing. You haven't worn that in years." He embraced her and placed a passionate kiss on her lips. A kiss that made her whole body ignite. No one could kiss quite like Jason James.

"I was hoping you'd say that." Delia smiled and licked her lips seductively. "Look," she said, grabbing his hand and

Chapter 1

pulling him toward the dining room, "I made a romantic meal for us. I've already eaten, but I thought you could eat and then we could go to the bedroom for ... dessert."

Delia sneezed. She didn't know why she was nervous. This was her husband. She shouldn't be nervous in front of her own husband. But the increasingly uncomfortable expression on Jason's face worried her. "What's wrong, honey?"

"Nothing," he said as he scratched his head. He let go of Delia's hand then rubbed the back of his neck. "It's just that, I had no idea you were planning any of this and I kind of brought company over."

"Company?"

"Yeah, the friend I was helping out, well, she needs a place to stay."

"She?"

"Gina," he called out into the hallway. In walked a beautiful, leggy, redhead carrying a suitcase extremely similar to the set Jason had bought for Delia on their second wedding anniversary.

Tears stung behind Delia's eyes, but she didn't have the energy to cry. It took all of her strength and thinking capabilities to just keep breathing. She felt cold all over as she stood nearly naked in front of a painstakingly arranged dinner table facing what was most likely her husband's latest conquest.

"Are you okay, Baby? You look a little ill."

"Do you want me to get her some water, Jay?" Delia's eyes expanded as she watched Gina walk straight to the kitchen, open a cabinet and retrieve a glass. How did she know where the glasses were? "Here you go," she said cheerily as she held out a glass of water to Delia.

She wanted to smack it out of her porcelain white hand, but she couldn't move. She couldn't even blink. She just stared. She stared at the beautiful redhead standing in her living room. And she really was beautiful. Delia touched her own mass of dark brown curls as she enviously noticed the perfectly coiffed cherry colored hair of Gina. She wondered what her own hair would look like in that color. She wondered if Jason would love her if her hair were that color.

Somehow she ended up on the dreaded couch wrapped in a blanket listening to some ridiculous story about how Jason and Gina were friends from work and Gina's roommate failed to pay the rent so she was being evicted and needed a place to stay. Delia stared at the lavish furnishings of their apartment. The coffee table trimmed with gold and crystal, the baby grand piano in the corner that no one played, the plasma television that rose from the floor. Everything seemed so hollow and empty.

"Delia, the car's running and I'm not leaving without you so — " Donna Lee stopped short when she entered the penthouse apartment and saw the situation.

"Gina, this is Delia's sister Donna," Jason offered after an awkward silence.

Donna Lee stared at Jason with a glare that could've melted his face. "I've known you for over four annoying years. You know good and well my name is Donna Lee. Call me Donna again and I'll kick you in the nuts."

Jason rolled his eyes and sighed. It was hard to tell with him whether he really forgot how much Donna Lee hated to be called Donna or whether he was just so disinterested in anything that didn't concern himself that it didn't strike him as necessary to remember.

"Sister? How can they be sisters? Delia's black and she's Chinese," Gina said with a perplexed look on her face.

Donna Lee crossed her arms and stepped toward the giant of a redhead. "First of all, I'm Korean not Chinese, you flat-chested, bird-brained, bitch. Second of all, what the hell are you doing in my sister's house?"

Chapter 1

Gina took a step back clearly intimidated by the petite Donna Lee. Jason stepped between them and said, "Donna Lee, watch your language. I won't tolerate you disrespecting my guests in my own home."

"Well, here's an idea Jason," Donna Lee said with sarcastic sweetness. "How about I not tolerate you disrespecting my sister anymore?"

"What goes on in this house is none of your business. We can solve our own problems."

The way Jason looked at both Gina and Delia when he said "we" made Donna Lee take a step back and survey the situation again. "What do you mean 'we'?" she asked with fierce skepticism. A tense silence fell over the room. Delia continued to stare blankly at the coffee table. Jason turned aside and rubbed the back of his neck. Gina chewed on her thumbnail and tried to blend into the background. "Would someone please tell me what's going on here?"

"I'm moving in, so technically, this is my home too," Gina volunteered with tentative confidence as she looked to Jason for support. He continued to avoid eye contact with anyone.

Donna Lee looked from Gina to Jason and back several times. "Why you son of a — " Donna Lee lunged for Jason and got a good punch in before he grabbed her wrists and restrained her. "How dare you? Are you out of your God damn mind?"

"It's not like that — " Jason protested as he easily picked up the petite Donna Lee and tossed her into a chair.

"The hell it ain't. Delia, get your stuff, we're leaving."

Delia didn't move. She couldn't move. She focused on her 3 inch Jimmy Choo's in order to keep from thinking about the insanity of the situation and passing out. She had about fifty pairs of heels in her overstocked closet. Jason still didn't think that was enough. He loved to see her in heels. Especially these particular heels. He thought they made her look ridiculously sexy. It was odd how her life was completely falling apart in front of her but all she could think about was shoes. She giggled to herself. She must have been losing her mind.

"Dee, what are you laughing at? Get your stuff. We are out," Donna Lee said.

A smile spread across Delia's face as another thought entered her mind. It had to do with what her sister said about Jason's nuts earlier.

Slowly she got to her feet as her smile spread wider and her giggle grew louder. Everyone in the room stared at her probably thinking she was having a nervous breakdown. After several moments, Delia finally stopped laughing. Then with all her might, she kicked her husband in the balls.

Chapter 2

Delia's life spiraled into an abyss of oblivion. Jason had left her with no marriage, no money, and no identity. Yes, no money. There was a prenuptial agreement, which she had signed against Donna Lee's adamant opinion. Worse than the lack of money was the lack of identity. After marrying Jason, she felt like she belonged to someone for the first time in her life. She had a name that she had chosen, not one that had been given to her. So, now, once again she felt trapped inside nothingness and she didn't know how to crawl out and find herself.

Immediately after the break-up, Delia moved in with Donna Lee and her two roommates, Shannon and Sharon. She didn't leave the couch for weeks as she wallowed in her failures. The longer she moped the more she failed. She lost her job as a research analyst for the National Science Institute. The only thing she succeeded in was annoying and imposing upon her sister and her two roommates.

"Delia, I love you, but this has got to end," Donna Lee said one evening as she came home from work.

Trying to block out the forthcoming nagging session, Delia rolled over on the couch and placed a pillow over her head.

"I was so proud of you when you kicked Jason in the nuts. I really thought you were gonna spring back from this, but apparently not. You've got to get yourself together. Jason was a no good creep. He's not worth all this. You've gotta get over him."

She didn't reply. Her sister just didn't understand. She had never been married. In fact, Delia couldn't think of a single relationship Donna Lee had ever had that lasted longer than two months.

"You know what your problem is? You've let Jason define you for so long you can't see yourself without him. You think because your biological parents didn't want you that no one could ever want you. One charismatic grin from that trouser troll and he had you thinking that you were the most beautiful you had ever been. Well, you know what, Delia? You are beautiful. With or without him."

Delia kept her head under the pillow to hide the tears that had developed from the all too true words of her adoptive sister. Deep down she knew Donna Lee was right. She knew she couldn't carry on sleeping on a couch and dwelling on her pathetic life. She had to find a way to get on with her life.

The next day, she made progress. She actually got off the couch for longer than twenty minutes and managed to put on an outfit that didn't closely resemble pajamas. As a way to say thank you to her current landlords, she took a few minutes to straighten up the apartment. For the first time she realized what a mess she'd been living in. Her sister and her roommates were complete pigs. They still lived as college students even though they had graduated three years ago. With pizza boxes stacked next to the door and home furnishings made of empty milk crates, Delia knew she definitely had to get out of that apartment as soon as possible. But the thought of finding her own place, a new job, and jumping back into the rigmarole of paying bills and just, well, living overwhelmed her.

Delia returned to the comfort and security of the couch. While massaging the bra strap indentations in her shoulder with one hand, she reached for the remote with the other. She really hated her huge breasts and longed for the day when she could afford to have the implants removed.

After clicking on the television, Delia searched for a show that didn't feature a man or a woman or love in any way, shape or form. She channel surfed for nearly an hour then settled on a program that showed the physics of roller coasters. Besides realizing that she was a complete nerd for enjoying something like that, she also realized that she had never been on a vacation. Even though it would probably drain the last of her savings, she felt it was something she needed to do.

With a newfound resolve and excitement for having a goal, Delia opened her laptop and started making plans.

"A cruise?" Donna Lee said, nodding. "I gotta say, that sounds like a great idea. I'm so proud of you." She gave Delia a big hug before opening the refrigerator and shaking her head in disappointment at the meager provisions. "Oh, and it'll give us an excuse to go clothes shopping," she said excitedly while reaching for a carton of leftover Chinese food.

She stuck her hand in and pulled out something that probably used to be broccoli. After sniffing it, she shrugged, tossed it in her mouth and said, "We gotta get you some sexy clothes. You dress like you're fifty, not twenty-five."

"Well, actually, that's perfect for this cruise."

***

The Golden Swan Cruise line was exactly what Delia wanted and needed. Considering that 90% of its passengers were over 70, she knew she wouldn't have to worry about men hitting on her. She could finally clear her head, relax, and try to find the good in herself.

The cruise started out perfectly except for a few of the feisty old men that would try to put the moves on her every once in a while. Delia always graciously declined their advances. The attention should have raised her self-esteem but it didn't. As far as she could tell, she was the only one on the boat with all her natural teeth. Of course they hit on her.

The only thing that bothered her was an alarmingly attractive young man she'd noticed when she boarded the boat. He was the only other passenger that seemed to be in his twenties as well. His short dark hair and penetrating blue eyes captivated her even from a distance.

After three days on the boat, she'd seen him a total of eleven times. She didn't know why she was counting. It just turned into a fun little game in her head. She would pick a spot on the boat and see how long it took before he passed by. Then she would sit back and study him. Delia told herself there was no harm in looking.

Tonight she found him in the ship's nightclub. But then again, he was there every night so really she found him without looking. Stealing an innocent glance, she noticed he was wearing a black fedora tipped to the side along with a precision pressed shirt and a skinny tie. She wondered why he always looked like he'd just stepped out of a revival of Guys and Dolls. Delia shook her head and returned her attention to her drink. She was becoming obsessed with a random stranger. Yet, he did not seem equally enthralled with her. Instead, he was completely captivated by a woman that had to be twice his age. He was obviously some sort of gigolo.

***

Chase Donovan stacked his beer bottle caps into a mini tower on the bar. When they toppled over, he started again.

"Another beer?" Jim the bartender asked.

Chapter 2

Chase counted the caps. He'd already had six, but he wasn't drunk. He never got drunk. His alarmingly high tolerance for alcohol was sometimes very annoying. He wished he was drunk. Maybe then he could tolerate Felicia flirting with every man in this stupid gaudy nightclub.

"Nah, I think I'll settle up and get out of here." Chase stood and stretched.

"You sure? Looks like Felicia's having a great time. I'm not sure she's ready to go yet."

Chase glanced at the dance floor and saw Felicia gyrating with not one, but two men. He rolled his eyes and sat back down. He knew he couldn't leave her there alone. He had to make sure she got back to her room safely.

Jim chuckled and placed another beer in front of Chase. "On the house," he said. "Why don't you try to enjoy yourself a little more?" he added while nodding to his left.

Chase knew what he was nodding toward. The pretty little dark-skinned girl with the green eyes who sat alone at the end of the bar night after night. Chase had admired her beauty from afar ever since the cruise left Florida. He'd even mentioned it to Jim but had been reluctant to approach her. He didn't take this cruise to pick up girls. He'd taken it for Felicia, but did she appreciate his sacrifice? He looked at the dance floor again and heard a resounding 'no' in his head.

He took a long swig of beer, tipped his hat to the perfect angle, then made his way over to her. He had to take a chance at some point. He was starting to see her eyes in his sleep. And if she rejected him, that would still be less embarrassing than what Felicia was currently doing on the dance floor.

"You've been nursing that martini for twenty minutes now," he said with uncharacteristic boldness. It must have been the seven beers talking.

"What? Oh, I'm not a big drinker," she said, looking at the glass of alcohol that had hardly been touched. "I don't

193

even know why I ordered this. I guess I figured since I was in a bar I might as well try to fit in."

"If you want to fit in here, you're going to have to break a hip," he said. She laughed the most enchanting, delicate, feminine, beautiful laugh he had ever heard. His pulse raced and his stomach fluttered, but maybe it was the alcohol. Yeah, it had to be the alcohol.

Chase smiled and searched for something else to say. Something to the effect of 'I think you're gorgeous and I'd like to get to know you better.' But that didn't sound right. It sounded desperate. He should have taken a few more minutes and worked out some pick up lines before he came over. Better yet, he should have texted Sammy and asked him what to say. Sammy always had the right words. Not like Chase. Chase was usually too busy to worry about women. So now here he was trapped. Standing in front of possibly the most beautiful woman he would ever see in his life, smiling like an idiot, and not having a clue as to what to say.

"Your eyes are beautiful," he blurted. Chase reddened and looked away. That was possibly the most juvenile line he could ever say. What was he thinking?

"Thank you very much for the compliment, but you can go back to your date now. What was her name? Felicia?"

"Felicia? Date? No, no, you're mistaken. We're not together ... well, we're together, but not like that."

"Look you don't have to explain it to me. But as someone that has been cheated on many ... many times, I know how it feels and I would never want to be a part of that. I'm not here to break up relationships."

"No, no seriously, you've got it wrong. She's my grandmother."

The beautiful woman furrowed her eyebrows as she looked from Chase to Felicia and back. "She looks a bit young to be your grandmother."

Chapter 2

"She looks good for her age, but I assure you, she's my grandmother." Chase reached into his pocket and pulled out a picture from his wallet. The picture showed a little boy about six years old being held by a tall blond woman who looked remarkably like Felicia. "We've taken this cruise every summer since I was eleven. It's our chance to bond."

"That is the sweetest thing I have ever heard in my life." She took the picture out of his hand and studied it more closely. "You are so lucky to be close with your grandmother. I would love to know my grandmother. Or any biological family for that matter. I'm Delia."

"Chase, Chase Donovan." He shook her hand and sat down next to her. "So why don't you know your family?"

***

"You ready to go, Son?" Felicia asked an hour later as she dried beads of sweat from her face with a handkerchief. Delia studied the woman's face and physique. She approximated Chase's age to be about 25, which meant that Felicia had to be around 65. Delia prayed she would look that good at 65. Felicia barely had a wrinkle and she had a light in her eyes that made her look almost juvenile. She reminded Delia of the ethereal Heather Locklear who never seemed to age.

"Not yet, Grandma. Why don't you go back to the room and I'll meet you there?"

"What did I tell you about calling me Grandma in public?" Felicia said in a forced whisper. "I'm trying to pass for 50 here. No one is going to believe that if they know I'm your grandmother." Then she kissed the side of his head and tousled his hair. "Are you going to introduce me to your friend?"

"Oh, sorry, this is Delia."

"Delia," Felicia repeated with a smile. "Beautiful name for a beautiful girl. Make my boy happy okay? He needs a good woman to straighten him out." Just then, a techno version of "Smoke Gets in Your Eyes" started playing. "Oh, I love this song," she said, clasping her hands.

With that, she was whisked away by a crowd of fawning suitors leaving Chase smiling after her.

***

At three o'clock in the morning, the glittery disco ball stopped turning. Chase and Delia looked around and noticed they were the only ones left in the nightclub. All the retirees had long gone to bed.

"Sorry kids, I gotta kick you out," Jim said as he reached for Delia's still half full martini glass.

Delia looked at her watch and felt completely embarrassed that she had just spent four and a half hours talking to a complete stranger in a bar. She just couldn't believe how easy it was to talk to him. She had been married to Jason for four years yet couldn't recall a time when they had spent more than thirty minutes talking. And the conversation was usually about him.

Chase, on the other hand, rarely spoke about himself. Instead, he just listened to Delia and even seemed interested in what she had to say. He found her former job with the National Science Institute fascinating and even asked questions about it. He laughed at her stories about Donna Lee, and the best part, he didn't stare at her breasts. Of course, with the shirt she had buttoned up to her neck, he wouldn't have seen much anyway.

"May I escort you to your room?" he asked, standing and reaching for her hand.

Feeling as if she were being courted by a gentleman, she felt herself flush. That simple question and the tiny gesture of him taking her hand nearly made her cry. For the first time in her life she felt … special.

He never relinquished her hand. She noted the unique way he held hands with her. It wasn't static or stationary. His hands continuously moved over and caressed hers as if he was a blind man trying to memorize the outline of her fingers and palms.

They walked hand in hand along the deck of the Golden Swan, staring out into the sea enjoying the warm summer breeze drifting from the coast of Barbados. They took the long route back to the cabins and even stopped along the way to play an impromptu moonlight game of shuffle board.

"How are you so good at this?" Delia squealed after missing her mark for the third time.

"Years of practice. I told you I'm on this boat every summer. Not only can I spank you in shuffle board, but I can also whip you in bridge, mahjong, and horseshoes." He smiled then said, "By the end of this cruise, you'll be able to hold your own. And by next year, I bet you'll be giving me a run for my money."

When they stopped in front of Delia's cabin to part ways, she realized she didn't want to part. Just the idea that she was attracted to a man other than Jason excited her. Not only was she attracted to him, but he seemed to like her as well. Maybe she wasn't as worthless as she thought.

***

Chase's heart nearly stopped when they reached Delia's door. He didn't want to leave her, but he also didn't want her to invite him in. Though he wanted her badly, he couldn't afford a relationship at this point in his life. But maybe it didn't have to be a relationship, maybe just a ... He shook that thought away. There was no way he could use her like that. After the night they'd had, the conversation, the long looks into her emerald eyes, he thought he might be ...well, he wasn't going to use the L word yet, but he did know that something very special had happened to him.

"Well, this is me," Delia said, nodding to the door.

"Right, of course," Chase jammed his hands into his creased black pants in order to resist the urge to scoop her up into his arms. "So, will I see you again?"

"Yeah, sure, do you want to do breakfast?"

"Yeah, sure."

Chase looked down at his shoes and kicked at an invisible stone like a shy teenager on his first date.

After Chase had kicked the invisible stone to death, he began to awkwardly pick the paint off the door frame as he waited for his confidence to surge and give him the needed boost to make a move. Finally, he took in a deep breath and said, "Can I kiss you now?"

After a cute, demure smile crept across her face, she nodded her head and he leaned in to claim his prize.

Chase teased her lips with two or three soft, endearing pecks before pressing his mouth firmly to hers. Then he wrapped his arm around her and brought her body so close to him that he could feel her heart racing. A warm, velvety tongue parted her full lips and began to slowly, tenderly and erotically probe the depths of her mouth. Delia moaned as she wrapped her arms around his neck and returned the passion of his kiss.

They stood there, lips and bodies locked, until they were both hot and breathless. Then, Chase remembered his position. This was not the time, he said to himself as he pulled away. For God's sake, she lived in D.C. What would happen if they met after the cruise?

"I better go," he breathed.

"Yeah, you better go," she repeated as if delirious.

He tasted her lips one more time before relinquishing his hold. Even after she'd closed the door behind her, he couldn't escape the image of her eyes, her smile and her lips. Chase rested his forehead on her door. What have I done? he thought.

Chapter 3

"Honestly, I think I was born in the wrong decade," Chase said two days later at lunch. "I mean, how cool would it be to live in a time when people got dressed up to go to the supermarket? Men wore suits and ties and hats and just looked sharp all the time."

Chase took a bag of nacho cheese Doritos and crumpled them all over his shrimp salad. Delia noticed he added Doritos to nearly every meal. At first she thought it was odd; now she thought it was one of his many adorable quirks.

"And the music. Don't get me started on the music. Frank Sinatra, Nat King Cole, Dean Martin, Perry Como, music that is timeless and just plain … beautiful."

He smiled and looked at Delia when he said the word 'beautiful' as if he was referring to her as well. Then he continued with endearing child-like exuberance as he said, "I mean, think about the music today. Are we going to be talking about it like this fifty years from now? Probably not. Young people today don't listen to music with such simple, pure, yet honest, relevant, and poetic lyrics."

Then suddenly, he was out of his seat and singing the lyrics to "Embraceable You". He took Delia's hand, stood her up and started swaying to the imaginary music and continued singing the incredibly romantic lyrics. He actually had a pretty good voice. Other people in the restaurant began to smile and stare at the two young lovers dancing around the tables to no music at all. Then someone sat at the piano and began musical accompaniment.

Chase wrapped his arms around her and dipped her. Normally, Delia would have been mortified with this sort of display. She would have needed to bring out her allergy medication for the fit of sneezes it would have caused, but something about Chase put her at ease. She just let herself relax and enjoy the moment. When he finished, the restaurant erupted in applause.

"There are two fatal flaws in your desire to return to the fifties and sixties," Delia said once they had sat back down to their lunch.

"Really, what?"

"Well, in the fifties, our relationship would not be accepted."

Chase knew she referred to their different races, but what struck him more was the fact that she thought they were in a relationship. He had already let it go too far.

"Do you have a problem with my race?" she asked, noticing a change in his demeanor.

"What? Oh, no, of course not. I couldn't care less that you're … Actually, I don't even know what race you are."

"Honestly, neither do I. Since I've never met my parents, there's no way I can be sure."

"Have you ever thought about trying to find them?"

"I wouldn't even know where to start. Besides, I wouldn't want to upset the only mother I've known. I don't want her to think she wasn't enough for me."

Chapter 3

"I can't imagine how hard it is for you not knowing where you come from."

Delia looked down at her plate and started pushing around the pasta noodles as she had suddenly lost her appetite.

"So what was the other fatal flaw?" he asked cheerfully, trying to lighten the mood.

"What? Oh, well," Delia reached across the table, grabbed the half-empty bag of chips and dumped the rest of the contents on top of her pasta. "In the fifties, no Doritos."

***

After lunch they went for a swim together in one of the ship's outdoor pools. Completely self-conscious of her body, including her freakishly large boobs, Delia sat on the edge of the pool still wearing her bathrobe as Chase splashed around her trying to convince her to jump in.

Now he had a great body, Delia thought. He was built kind of like a soccer player with well-defined muscles, but nothing over the top. His muscles were natural, long, and lean. Not like Jason, who would spend hours a week in the gym, tanning beds, and waxing salons searching for that hunky look. It was a look that was attractive to the majority of women. Jason could take off his shirt and women would faint. For Delia, however, his beauty rituals wore her thin and made her feel even more inadequate about her body. Somehow Chase's body turned her on even more than Jason's did.

Looking around the pool didn't help her self-consciousness. She felt she stuck out too much. There were sixty and seventy-year-old women strutting around in bikinis letting their wrinkles hang in all their glory. Meanwhile she was sitting there with a 34D bust and a 26 inch waist afraid to show her modest one piece for fear she'd look like a cartoon character.

After pleading with her several times to join him in the water, Chase decided to take matters into his own hands. He swam up to her innocently then grabbed her by the legs and dunked her underwater, bathrobe and all. Delia squealed and tried to kick herself free.

Her kicking and squirming proved fruitless as he was much too strong for her. After a few moments, she relaxed in the water and let him hold her.

"You're beautiful," he whispered in her ear.

The weight of the bathrobe soon tired her so she took it off and laid it by the side of the pool.

***

Even though they had spent every waking moment together —even a few non-waking moments —for the past few days, he had never seen her in anything revealing. He loved her modesty. She reminded him of the classy women of the forties and fifties. But when she took off her robe and he got a glimpse of her true figure, he gasped. She was simply breathtaking. He had to control his manly urge to grope her right there in public.

***

Feeling a little guilty for monopolizing all of Chase's time, Delia suggested he spend the afternoon with his grandmother. Well, the real reason for the suggestion was that she wanted some time alone to shop for the perfect dress for their last night on the ship. She wished she had taken Donna Lee up on her offer to go shopping before she left DC. But she hadn't anticipated meeting someone like Chase. He was absolutely the right guy at the right time. She didn't feel insecure or invisible when she was with him. She just felt … alive.

While looking through the clothing racks at Becky's, the ship's dress boutique, she tried to imagine what Donna Lee would want her to wear. In fact, she wondered what Donna Lee would do if she were about to go dancing possibly for the last time with a handsome perfect stranger. She didn't have to wonder too hard. Delia had memories of detailed Donna Lee exploits and one night stands. She never remembered her beautiful, confident sister ever crying over a guy. Maybe that wasn't such a bad way to live, she thought.

***

Every night ended the same way. After dancing the evening away in one of the ship's nightclubs, they would stroll along the deck and talk for hours then kiss in front of Delia's door. Chase told himself that as long as he didn't let it go any farther he'd be fine. He wasn't too attached and he could leave the ship with no strings. In a few days or weeks he'd get over her. He looked down at the sexy black cocktail dress she wore. Okay, maybe months.

"I'm not wearing underwear," Delia giggled, suddenly snapping Chase out of his thoughts about how to end their romance. She rested her head onto his chest and nestled closer to him as they slow danced to "Bewitched" by Frank Sinatra. His whole body tightened as he resisted the urge to run his hands over the smooth curve of her butt.

"Did you hear me? I'm not wearing any underwear." Delia lifted her head and kissed the bottom of Chase's chin. Then she kissed down his neck to the top of his chest, sending a thrill throughout his body that landed in his loins.

"Delia, I think you've had too much to drink." For the first time in a week, he had seen her drink more than two sips of an alcoholic beverage. That night at dinner, she'd had not one, but two glasses of wine and he could see the effect it had on her.

"You're probably right. But that doesn't change the fact that I'm not wearing underwear, does it?" she said in a singsong voice before giggling again.

He had tried to be a perfect gentleman all week. He had tried not to get too close to her even though their make-out sessions in front of her door lasted longer and longer each night. He only let the conversation dwell on superficial things, especially after he learned that she too was from Washington D.C. Even though Delia had revealed so much about her life including her sister, her failed marriage, even about being adopted, Chase hadn't revealed anything about himself.

All she knew about him was that he and his grandmother were very close. Anytime Delia wanted to know more about him, he expertly directed the conversation toward the topic of Felicia or to his fascination with the fifties. He'd played it as careful as he could, knowing the feelings that were developing in him and knowing that if she found out the truth about him, she would probably run away screaming.

"Maybe we should go," Delia said dejectedly after she received no response from him. She pulled away and ran her fingers over her long hair which she had recently straightened.

"Delia, I — "

"No, it's okay. I don't know what came over me. I'm so embarrassed." She turned and dashed out of the nightclub.

He had to be discreet. He had to use discretion.

"Delia, I just don't want to take advantage of you," he said once he caught up with her in the hallway.

"Chase, I'm a grown woman. I know what I'm doing."

Discreet. Discretion.

"But there's a lot you don't know about me. I don't want to hurt you."

"This has been the most romantic week of my life, Chase. I just wanted … I just thought … "

He sealed her lips with a kiss that made her melt in his arms. They stumbled around the corridor until he had her pinned against a wall. His hands caressed the silky contours of her dress until they reached her glorious panty-less bottom.

Screw discretion …

End of Sample

www.ingramcontent.com/pod-product-compliance
Lightning Source LLC
Chambersburg PA
CBHW030322180626
46810CB00003B/1195